"What do you need from me?"

"To portray his wife," Crew said, tossing a thumb at Hunter.

Eden blinked. "Oh." She swung her gaze to Hunter, trying to read his expression and failing to pierce that icy stare. "A husband? That ought to be a tough role for you."

"This is strictly business."

"I never assumed otherwise." She said it with such dignity, with such complete aplomb, that Hunter experienced a jab somewhere around his heart.

"Let me explain the situation before you agree."

"That's really not necessary, Agent Crew. I'm aware of what portraying a wife entails. Make it look real, live together. Behave in a loving manner? I'm sure Officer Couviyon has told you that I'd agreed to be his wife several years ago." Her gaze slid to Hunter's.

"Then do it again," Hunter said. "Be my wife, Eden." The soul dropped out of his heart, like it had when he'd said those words once before. "Help me catch a killer."

Dear Harlequin Intrigue Reader,

To chase away those end-of-summer blues, we have an explosive lineup that's guaranteed to please!

Joanna Wayne leaves goosebumps with *A Father's Duty*, the third book in NEW ORLEANS CONFIDENTIAL. In this riveting conclusion, murder, mayhem...and mystique are unleashed in the Big Easy. And that's just the beginning! *Unauthorized Passion*, which marks the beginning of Amanda Stevens's new action-packed miniseries, MATCHMAKERS UNDERGROUND, features a lethally sexy lawman who takes a beautiful imposter into his protective custody. Look for *Just Past Midnight* by Ms. Stevens from Harlequin Books next month at your favorite retail outlet.

Danger and discord sweep through Antelope Flats when B.J. Daniels launches her western series, McCALLS' MONTANA. Will the town ever be the same after a fiery showdown between a man on a mission and *The Cowgirl in Question*? Next up, the second book in ECLIPSE, our new gothic-inspired promotion. *Midnight Island Sanctuary* by Susan Peterson—a spine-tingling "gaslight" mystery set in a remote coastal town—will pull you into a chilling riptide.

To wrap up this month's thrilling lineup, Amy J. Fetzer returns to Harlequin Intrigue to unravel a sinister black-market baby ring mystery in *Undercover Marriage*. And, finally, don't miss *The Stolen Bride* by Jacqueline Diamond— an edge-of-your-seat reunion romance about an amnesiac bride-in-jeopardy who is about to get a crash course in true love.

Enjoy!

Denise O'Sullivan
Senior Editor
Harlequin Intrigue

UNDERCOVER MARRIAGE

AMY J. FETZER

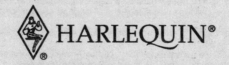

HARLEQUIN®

TORONTO • NEW YORK • LONDON
AMSTERDAM • PARIS • SYDNEY • HAMBURG
STOCKHOLM • ATHENS • TOKYO • MILAN • MADRID
PRAGUE • WARSAW • BUDAPEST • AUCKLAND

ISBN 0-373-22799-X

UNDERCOVER MARRIAGE

Copyright © 2004 by Amy J. Fetzer

All rights reserved. Except for use in any review, the reproduction or
utilization of this work in whole or in part in any form by any electronic,
mechanical or other means, now known or hereafter invented, including
xerography, photocopying and recording, or in any information storage
or retrieval system, is forbidden without the written permission of the
publisher, Harlequin Enterprises Limited, 225 Duncan Mill Road,
Don Mills, Ontario, Canada M3B 3K9.

All characters in this book have no existence outside the imagination of
the author and have no relation whatsoever to anyone bearing the same
name or names. They are not even distantly inspired by any individual
known or unknown to the author, and all incidents are pure invention.

This edition published by arrangement with Harlequin Books S.A.

® and TM are trademarks of the publisher. Trademarks indicated with
® are registered in the United States Patent and Trademark Office, the
Canadian Trade Marks Office and in other countries.

www.eHarlequin.com

Printed in U.S.A.

ABOUT THE AUTHOR

Amy J. Fetzer was born in New England and raised all over the world. She uses her own experiences in creating the characters and settings for her novels. Married more than twenty years to a United States marine, and the mother of two sons, Amy covets the moments when she can curl up with a cup of cappuccino and a good book.

Books by Amy J. Fetzer

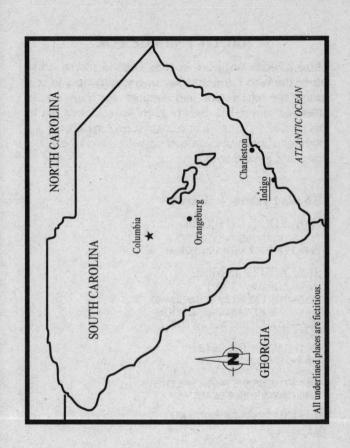

NORTH CAROLINA

SOUTH CAROLINA

GEORGIA

ATLANTIC OCEAN

Columbia

Orangeburg

Charleston

Indigo

N

All underlined places are fictitious.

CAST OF CHARACTERS

Eden Carlyle—Eden's search for her murdered sister's missing infant puts her in grave danger and, brings her face-to-face with the man who betrayed her love.

Hunter Couviyon—Seven years ago he left his family and the woman he loved for a high-risk CIA job. Now he's tracked a black-market baby ring that's brought him back into Eden's life…for good?

Roxanne Mitchell—The attorney has her hands in the adoption business, but just how legal is her representation?

Duke Pastori—Rock-star handsome, he was a comfort to young, pregnant women. But could he be an accomplice to their murders?

Margaret Harker—Like her mother and grandmother before her, Margaret helps couples adopt the baby of their dreams. But could she be their worst nightmare?

Harris Bruiner—Handsome and distinguished, he evokes trust and sympathy, but does he use his charm to lure and kill innocent women?

Paulette and Chase Ramsgate—Young, wealthy, old money—they want a baby and are willing to do anything for the chance at parenthood…but even commit murder?

For Cherry Adair.

When we were young we wanted lots of friends,
When we grew older, we chose them carefully.
True friends are rare and precious,
the kind that come into your life
and leave a lasting impression.

You're one of them.

Thanks for being there.

'Amy-belle'

Prologue

He was gaining on her, calling to her that she was too weak and to come back; he'd take care of her. But he wouldn't. He'd kill her. There was no question in Helene's mind.

Her bare feet pounded on the soft, damp earth, the night and forest closing around her like a misty blanket. Her legs were like rubber, muscles soft, and when she chanced a look behind herself, she fell. She wanted to stay there and give up. She was so weak and tired, but she wasn't about to go down like a wimp and scrambled to her feet, running. She didn't have a choice.

If she stopped, she would die.

Branches and broken saplings ripped at her skin, blood already trailing down her legs. Helene held her stomach and pain swallowed more of her strength. She heaved for air, straining the unused muscles that had carried a baby for nine months.

A baby she'd never held. A baby he'd stolen from

her as it drew its first breath. A daughter. That much she remembered in spite of the drugs.

She had no idea where she was, how close to the city, or how far. She only knew that he was going to kill her. She heard him, his heavy feet thumping against the ground with determination. And he called to her, in that voice she'd loved—the one he'd used to betray her.

What had they done with her baby?

They said it was dead. Her little girl was dead.

But he'd lied to her so much, she didn't believe in anything anymore. He'd pampered her, let her love him and feel loved. Lies. All of it. She was nothing more than a baby machine.

She saw car lights flare in the distance and raced toward them. She'd hail someone, she'd risk anything to stay alive and find her child. She reached the road, the car long gone and the road empty and wet. Still clutching her stomach, she felt a tearing inside her as she stepped onto the road, gasping for air and waving her arms to an oncoming car. The bright headlights flashed on her. The car kept coming right for her, and when she thought it would slam into her, it jerked to a stop. The shock sent her backward and she hit the ground. Everything hurt. Every muscle, bone, her heart. A man climbed out of the passenger side, silhouetted in the headlights.

She recognized him before he said, "You didn't think it would be that easy, did ya?"

She scrambled back and tried to stand, yet the

minute she did stand and turned to run, something hit her between the shoulders. She dropped face-first, her chin smacking on the asphalt. She felt her jaw shift and blood pour into her mouth.

Strong hands gripped her legs, dragging her back, dragging her across the road and into the woods. The soft grassy ground was a relief after the harsh gravel. Grabbing for roots, her hand closed around a rock. When he flipped her over, her vision swam. He bent to her, smiling tenderly and, with all the strength left in her, she cracked the rock against his head. He howled and staggered, and when she rolled to her side to get to her feet, the other man, the driver, clipped her in the back of the skull, and she went down again.

Then her lover came back with a vengeance. He backhanded her, smashing her broken jaw, sending starbursts of pain through her brain and still she fought. She wanted to live. She wanted her baby. She wanted this man to die. He straddled her, his weight pinning her to the ground. The pressure took her breath, pushed on her torn belly till she thought she'd explode.

She couldn't scream, already choking on her blood, so she kicked and clawed his face, his clothes, ripping his face, his suit pocket.

The other man stood by, jiggling car keys, waiting for her to die.

Her world shrank, her vision turning to a soft glow around the edges of her lover's face.

He smiled, handsome in the night. "Now, honey, is that any way to treat daddy?"

Then he withdrew a knife and inside, Helene silently screamed for her baby, for her sister, Eden, for the life she wanted to live and the mistakes that had brought her here—in the moonlight with a madman.

He pressed the blade point to her jugular and kissed her bloodstained mouth. Then almost gently, he pushed the steel into her skin.

Chapter One

Someone was selling babies.

Parceling up innocent fragile newborns like mail packages and offering them to people who were willing to pay a fortune for a child. And they were killing the mothers to do it.

Hunter Couviyon was here to put an end to it. He strolled through the gala ball at the Magnolia Plantation, weaving his way between the city's wealthiest patrons and nodding to the other guests, blending in and yet avoiding conversation. He made a career out of not being seen, masquerading as everything from a prince to an international weapons dealer. Anything it took, he thought, and this time, he was portraying a wealthy Southerner whose fortune was in pine timber.

The apple doesn't fall far from the tree, he thought, knowing he'd have become an actual timber magnate if he'd stayed in Indigo and followed the family tradition like his brother Logan. But he hadn't, and tonight his latest mission had brought him to a charity ball in Charleston. Everyone was suspect. Everyone was a lead to a killer.

He listened, watched, picked up bits of conversation and hoped for a clue. The rich were buying babies, and the rich were gathered in this grand ballroom.

Of all the assignments he'd taken, this one had crawled beneath his skin and locked inside him somewhere. He'd ignored the things he'd done and seen for years, but this time he was home, less than two hundred miles from his ancestral plantation, from his family and from memories he didn't want to relive.

But they came anyway; the faces of his family, and the anger and disappointment when he'd left seven years ago flooded back with lethal intensity, snatching at his mind and concentration. Being stateside after all this time felt like an explosion waiting to happen, except that no one knew he was here. And he planned to keep it that way.

He stepped through French doors on the side of the ballroom onto the side veranda, opened a silver cigarette case and lit a smoke he didn't want. It was an easy cover to study people. Most people didn't smoke, so there was no one to join him in the shadows. From here, he could see the ballroom and the driveway leading to the front doors. The perfect surveillance position.

On the street, limousines deposited the city's wealthy under the covered walk. The charity ball was already in full swing, the latecomers making a grand entrance in their finest. Inside, uniformed waiters passed silently through the crowds with French champagne and Russian caviar.

There was an irony about people who dressed up and ate beluga to the tune of a thousand dollars a pop in the name of charity. To him, it was a careless effort, a chance to be seen and to be thought of as a philanthropist. They'd have made a more worthwhile contribution if they'd stood on the giving end of a soup kitchen. He'd grown up around this kind of wealth, but at least his father had rolled up his sleeves and worked alongside the homeless and needy instead of throwing money at them and counting it off on his taxes.

His father's image burst into his mind, but before he lost his focus, he shoved it back into the archives of his brain and watched.

Hunter was here almost by accident. He'd stumbled on the black-market baby peddlers while infiltrating female slave-traders in Istanbul. He'd tracked the baby ring from Europe to the U.S., learning that along with buying nubile young virgins as slaves, anyone with enough money could buy a newborn baby. An American baby. Hunter didn't want to think about what the criminals who were heartless enough to sell girls into a life of misery and degradation would do to a helpless baby.

A newborn infant was as innocent as a victim could get.

The U.S.A. was federal territory, FBI jurisdiction. He'd been called in because the trail was international now, and he had some expertise with the ring in Europe. Adding to that, a U.S. senator's daughter was missing, pregnant, and had last been seen here, in Charleston. Senator Crane was an old college frat brother, and he'd cashed in his chips with the CIA director and asked Hunter to look for his daughter, Alice. The feds weren't happy about it, but Hunter didn't give a damn. They were all after the same prize and he didn't care who he had to walk over to get it. America's children weren't for sale.

Hunter's gaze zeroed in on a couple in their midthirties, the Ramsgates, remembering that he'd overheard them discussing adoption as he'd passed them. Nice place to start. He dropped the smoke and ground it beneath his heel, his gaze flicking inside the club, then jerking back again.

He moved through the open doors, the music and conversation rising with the blood suddenly rushing in his head.

One look at the redhead in a blue gown and his control slipped.

My God.

Eden?

EDEN CARLYLE'S GAZE skipped from one person to the next. The guests at the charity ball looked only happy and rich. Really rich. Heck, that woman's necklace would pay off the mortgage on her café. She couldn't imagine how her sister, Helene, knew anyone in these circles. Helene had been a college student, for pity's sake. Nearly penniless. Who would have given her the invitation to such a luxurious ball?

Eden sighed, a dozen questions without answers tumbling in her mind. She couldn't put the pieces together, and she didn't know exactly how she'd manage it, but she would solve the puzzle. She owed it to her little sister.

She needed to know why Helene had been murdered. Why she hadn't confided in her only living relative about the baby she'd carried. The thought of an innocent baby—her sister's child—lost somewhere pierced through the armor she'd kept as close as a shield. Her throat tightened around a hard lump and she swallowed back tears. She'd already shed a river of them in the last three weeks. The coroner had said Helene had given birth only a day or two before her murder, yet there was no trace of her baby, no records of the birth. No clues. A dead end.

Eden refused to believe it.

What did she know about investigating a crime? She owned a café! She'd already hired her friend and private investigator Hope Randell months ago when Helene had first broken off contact. Aside from the invitation she'd found in a box of Helene's things her old dorm mate had kept, Helene had left behind too little to help the police solve her murder. What there was was too old to be useful. Before her death, her sister had quite simply disappeared.

Eden closed her eyes for a second, trying to forget identifying her sister's body on a slab in the morgue. She tried to forget hearing the details of how her younger sister had been brutally beaten and stabbed and left in a shallow grave for wild animals to find. Anger rose in her, punching at her heart and heating her blood.

In one day, she'd lost her sister and the baby. She wanted Helene's killer to suffer as he'd made her sister suffer. She wanted someone to pay. It was the reason she was in this unfamiliar territory—in the middle of the Magnolia Plantation with people who tossed away huge sums of money to charity as if they were handing tips to St. Peter to get into heaven.

There was a risk that she'd open the wrong can of worms, but Eden had to do something. Find something. The invitation was her only lead. She'd let Helene put distance between them, let her sister down, and Eden blamed herself for being more of a mother to Helene than a friend. She wasn't going to let grass grow under her again.

The baby was all Eden had left in the world.

Taking a sip of expensive champagne, Eden's gaze toured the grand ballroom, the uniformed waiters, the band, the tuxedo-clad men and the women in designer gowns and enough diamonds to require bodyguards.

Old money, she thought, then realized one thing.

Someone was watching her. As if a fingertip slid down her spine, her skin prickled with awareness. Eden's gaze floated over the crowd, but other than the two men ogling her sheer top, no one was staring directly. She shifted, trying not to be obvious, bringing the champagne flute to her lips. A striking blond man approached her, smiling, and Eden braced herself for the lies she'd tell to learn more about her sister's life. The man drew closer, holding out his hand.

"I'm David Winston—" his gaze did a quick up and down "—and you take my breath away."

"Should I call for help?" she said, smiling and, surprisingly, not minding the heated way he looked at her. She offered her hand, only to be rudely blocked by another man in a tuxedo.

"Darlin', I was wondering where you'd gone off to."

Eden looked up and felt a hard punch to her lungs. *Oh, no.* "Hunter," came out in a whisper. What on earth was *he* doing here? Oh, she didn't want this, didn't need to be staring into those ice-blue eyes right now. Not after all this time.

"Excuse me," Winston said, scowling and inching closer. "We were making introductions."

"Not today." Hunter's gaze ripped over Eden as he shifted, putting his back to the man. She looked spectacular, more beautiful than he remembered.

When he'd first seen her, he'd thought he was

mistaken, but it was the way she moved that told him it was her. Graceful. And piles of dark-red hair. He'd seen her from behind, her slender spine exposed in the low-riding blue skirt that looked heavy, fishtailing behind her when she moved. His gaze dropped to a hand-width of tanned skin exposed between the top and bottom of the two-piece blue gown. It rode so low on her hips he could see her navel. And he remembered tasting that sweet little dent. The top wasn't any less provocative. Long-sleeved, it was dangerously sheer, offering the shape of her body and barely hanging on her shoulders, exposing the tops of her breasts. Hell, she might as well be naked except for the strategically placed beading over sheer fabric.

Eden frowned, Hunter's study too intense, too possessive. "You're being rude, Hunter."

His attention snapped back to her face. "Sorry, dear, I missed you."

"And lying, too." She arched a tapered brow. "Nothing new there."

Her words bit, and Hunter had to think fast, sliding his arm possessively around her waist, he whispered, "Don't talk." He glanced at the man who was looking at Eden as if he was waiting his turn to devour her. "Sorry, pal." He ushered Eden toward the patio doors.

"Get the hell away from me, Hunter." Eden's voice was low and furious, but she didn't want to make a scene in front of the very people she needed to pump for information on Helene. She pushed off his arm. It didn't work.

"Behave."

"Drop dead." Eden kept her smile plastered in place.

"Calm down, we're attracting attention."

"Then I suggest you let me go."

He didn't and instead, swept her onto the dance floor. She was stiff and unyielding in his arms, her beautiful green eyes flashing with outrage.

It was exciting to see. She kept her dignity in place, but those eyes told him it wouldn't last. She danced, her lush body a whisper from his, making his blood simmer and bringing memories. Memories of tasting her, of the sweet scent of her skin that drove him wild, of pushing into her body and feeling her close tightly around him, fitting him. Pulling him back to her.

Oh, man.

He wasn't going to be able to do his job tonight if he wasn't careful. He shoved aside the distracting emotions Eden was stirring inside him. "You have no idea the trouble you're starting," he said with a look that told the rest of the room that he was saying something else entirely. "Smile."

Eden laid her hand on his broad shoulder and smiled up at him. It was more like a tigress baring her fangs before the kill. And she was ready to bite.

"Good girl."

"When you walked out on me seven years ago,

Hunter, I was a girl. In case you didn't notice, I'm not a kid anymore."

Oh, he'd noticed all right. Seeing her here had seized him in the gut so hard he'd just stared, mesmerized. Seven years ago she'd been reserved, soft spoken, and dressed plainly. Now, she was she-cat sexy, vibrant and sleek, the blue beaded gown merely artfully draped fabric, exposing and hiding enough of her figure to give him hot dreams for weeks. Coupled with the waterfall of deep red hair spilling down her back, he was surprised half the men in the place weren't surrounding her. And then they had. He'd counted no less than six who'd spotted her two heartbeats after he had. It was good thing he could move fast because she had no idea how dangerous it was to be here. Dangerous to both of them.

The carefully placed cards in a house of deception were about to fall if he didn't do something. He danced closer, keeping his voice low. "It's not good for you to be here."

"How do you figure?" When he didn't answer, simply staring, she said, "Whatever ideas you have, I'm not your problem."

"You are now." If he didn't get her out of here, she'd blow his cover. Plans had already been set into motion. He danced her to the edge of the floor near the doors.

"I don't want to have anything to do with you again, Hunter."

His expression tightened. "You can ream me all you want, Eden, just not here, not now. Let's go." He steered her off the dance floor and toward the exit.

At the foyer, David Winston walked up to them. "Is there a problem?" His gaze flicked between them.

"No," Hunter said, impatient to be out of here before his cover turned to dust.

"I was asking *her.*" Winston looked at Eden.

Hunter looked down at her, waiting.

Eden debated whether or not to use this man as a barrier between her and Hunter. But the look Hunter tossed the man was enough to make Winston step back. It was so dangerously savage Eden felt a chill trip down her spine. It made her see how much he'd changed, how much she didn't know about him. Seven years was a very long time. This man wasn't even close to the one she used to love.

Her gaze slid to David Winston. "No, David, I'm fine. We're well acquainted." She laid her hand over Hunter's heart and inched closer. Two could play this game, she thought.

Hunter looked at her sharply, she didn't have to meet his gaze to know. She felt it. "We've had a…disagreement and he was tripping over himself to apologize."

Enough, Hunter thought. "Excuse us." He steered her across the foyer, taking her purse and pulling out her coat-check ticket. She was silent, her expression passive as he dropped the cloak over her shoulders and hailed the valet for his car. A few minutes later, the driver skidded to a halt and still she hadn't said a word, hadn't looked at him.

But he could feel her anger hovering around her like a dark vapor. He was almost looking forward to seeing her explode. He opened the door, yet she stood on the curb, her gaze so venomous it stung.

He stepped closer. "Get in."

"And if I don't?"

"I don't want to force you, Eden." He put his hand at the small of her back, giving her a push. "But I will."

She edged away. "I'm going because I don't want to make a scene here." She slid around the edge of the door and into the black sedan. "But I do plan to make a scene."

She was a lady, a Southern one. They had strict rules about public displays and Eden had been raised with all of them. She wouldn't make a scene in public. But alone, he wasn't sure. Not anymore. This woman was as different now as he was. Hunter's gaze lingered on her long legs as she pulled them inside, then he slammed the door. Walking around, he tipped the valet and slid behind the wheel. He leaned forward and removed the weapon from the holster at his back, setting it on the console between them.

Eden's gaze landed on the gun, then shot to him. "Just what have you been doing for the past seven years, Hunter?"

He didn't speak, putting the car in gear and driving away, fast.

"That's some cannon. Perhaps I *should* have made a scene."

He gave her a long slow look. Just the sight of her, her scent, touched off emotions he'd buried with everything else. He looked ahead and drove in silence, heading to privacy, to his hotel, where he'd have to tell her something, anything but the truth. The last place he wanted to be was alone in a room with Eden Carlyle.

The only woman he'd ever loved.

And the only woman he'd ever betrayed.

EDEN'S BRAIN WAS FUZZY.

Hunter was beside her, in a tux, with a gun, driving her God knew where, and she was going with him.

And she'd thought asking questions at the party was dangerous?

Eden glanced to the side. The darkness of the car shadowed Hunter's features, cloaking him in secrecy. Why she'd let him rush her from the party where she'd hoped to get information eluded her. Shock? Fear? Studying him, she noticed definite changes: his features were sharper, his eyes colder.

He spared her a quick glance and her stomach lurched. Well, some things never fade. It irritated her. And damn if the man hadn't aged well, too. He seemed bigger in the shoulders, but that could be the black tuxedo and a good tailor. Her gaze strayed to his hands gripping the steering wheel. Big, strong hands. She'd always loved his hands. Warm. Gentle. Smoothing over her skin. Eden looked away.

So not good. She was still reeling from that moment, the fraction of a second when she'd looked up and those ice-blue eyes had been gazing down at her. Time had slipped back, matchsticks of memory had flamed. Suddenly, it was the first time they'd kissed, made love by the river, then the day he'd claimed to love her and asked her to spend her life with him. She'd been deliriously happy. But a couple months later, when she was buying her wedding gown and selecting flowers, he'd left her. Humiliated her. She let the memories dissolve and gathered back the pain and embarrassment she'd suffered and forgotten, burying it deep inside her. It would be the only thing to keep her from screaming "why" at him right now.

She wouldn't give him the satisfaction.

"Why don't you just say what you want to, Eden?"

His deep voice punched the silence and made her flinch.

"No, thank you. I'd like your full attention for that, if you don't mind."

Hunter smiled to himself. She was always so damn polite. And she was nervous. He could tell because she sat perfectly still, yet her gaze darted all over the place. But that's all that resembled the woman he'd left behind—the woman he'd betrayed. And he hadn't stuck around to see the damage he'd done. Guilt pricked him like tiny needles, and his hands tightened on the steering wheel. He needed her gone, far and fast.

"Where are we going?"

"My hotel room."

She looked at him sharply, and that cynical little curl pulled at his lips. She didn't like it. A few moments later, he pulled up in front of the Omni Hotel. He stuffed the gun back in its holster. She'd almost forgotten about it and wondered if he was a cop like his brother Nash. The valet rushed forward, but Hunter was out of the car and opening her door before the young man could do it. As if he didn't want anyone near her. He looked down at her, offering his hand. She ignored it; it was petty, but she didn't want to touch him again.

She was done with Hunter. She'd made herself get over him, made herself move on. She'd been damn proud of herself, too. But now she felt as if it was all just window dressing. He was back, and she was hurting all over again.

Chapter Two

Hunter followed Eden to the elevator, admiring the sway of her hips and wondering where all the sexy elegance had come from. Last time he'd seen her, she'd been more unassuming, preferring not to be noticed. And despite the fact that her parents had been killed by a drunk driver, leaving a twenty-one-year-old woman to raise her kid sister, she'd had a smile for everyone. Mostly back then, those smiles had been for him.

The elevator doors hushed closed and the small confines brought everything about her into his awareness: the length and vibrant color of her hair, the inches of bare, tanned stomach above the hip-hugging skirt, and that delicious-looking navel it exposed. She'd been pretty before, now she was downright exotic, and the allure of her was tempting him to test the waters and be bad. Very bad. With her.

Eden glanced at him and snapped an irritated, "What? You're staring."

His gaze prowled over her, knowing what was

beneath that gown and aching to see it again. "You've changed."

"It's been seven years, what did you expect?"

Hunter hadn't considered her in a while. If he had, he wouldn't have been able to do what he'd wanted, needed, because just her image could destroy his concentration. But being with her, feeling her anger, brought back waves of regret and guilt. When he'd left, it had rested like a stone in his chest. He'd grown accustomed to the weight of it, knowing he'd willingly hurt her. It had nearly killed him to think about it. So he hadn't. "You look fantastic, baby."

The husky sound of Hunter's voice sent little needles of pleasure shooting through her. Eden smashed them down, mentally berating herself for wanting his compliments. She hadn't been good enough for him all those years ago, what was the difference now? She was the same person, right? Even as the thought fell through her confused mind, she knew it wasn't true. She wasn't the same, she'd never be the same.

"Thank you. You look…" She faced him, bracing her shoulder on the elevator wall. "A little tired, but good."

Hunter rubbed his hand over his mouth, tugged at the collar of his stark, white shirt. Just having him stare at her did crazy things to her body. "What were you doing at that party?" he asked.

"I had an invitation."

His expression said "yeah right" and before she

could say something that would definitely have been snide, the doors sprang open. He waited for her to exit. "Down there," he said, gesturing to the door at the far end of the hall as they walked. He opened the door, the scent of fresh flowers and clean, cool air coating her. She stepped inside and turned as he shut the door.

He faced her. "Well, let's have it. Fire at will."

The silence stretched, gazes clashing like thunder and blue lightning.

Eden wanted to slap him but since she'd never hit anyone before she wasn't about to sink low and start now. "Why should I? You mean nothing to me now." Saying it didn't give her the satisfaction she'd hoped. Because it was a lie. Her heart still ached just looking at him again.

Hunter stood rock still, something inside him breaking. "I knew that already. I had it coming, I guess."

"You guess?" Did he just forget what he did to her, soften it up in his mind over the years? "You know, I don't want to discuss our past with you now. How about you tell me why you're here, why you were at that party?"

"I'm not at liberty to say."

"Well, that's a very nice official response. Try again."

He didn't say a word.

"The point of bringing me here is what then?"

"To keep you out of my way."

She was in his way, a ball and chain to his plans. That's what she'd been before. "Fine. I'll make an effort to stay clear of you." She headed to the door.

He caught her arm. Her venomous gaze dropped to his touch. He let her go. "I can't allow you to go back to that party."

"Allow me?" Her already high temper rose another fraction. "You have a say in my life?"

"This isn't about us, Eden."

"Who said anything about *us?* I learn from my mistakes." She looked him over. "Apparently you still have trouble expressing yourself."

"Dammit, Eden. I'm not getting into this with you right now. I don't have time."

So what else was new? Then she thought for a second. "You didn't want anyone at that party to know we knew each other, why?"

He hesitated, then gave a little. "I'm working on something, and you being at that party and knowing me would destroy it."

"Undercover, were you?"

His features tightened.

"For whom?"

He didn't answer that and instead asked, "Why were you there?"

Satisfied they were getting somewhere, she moved into the living room. The suite was enormous, doors leading to other rooms circling the edge and the windows offering a view of the city. "I told you, I had an invitation."

"It's a grand a ticket."

"No, an invitation, not an obligation. It was Helene's. She's dead." Her eyes burned with the same angry heat they'd had since she'd received the call. "She was murdered."

"I'm sorry, Eden. God, I'm sorry." He reached for her.

She backed away, flinging her hands up as to stop him. "Don't. Don't say anything." Her hands fell listlessly to her sides. "You don't have to be sorry. It's not your fault."

Eden hunched her shoulders and kept her back to him as Hunter remembered her sister, years younger and rebellious as hell. While Eden had toed the line and behaved, Helene had been wild, piercing body parts, turning her red hair purple and wearing enough black to outfit a rock band. The last time Hunter had seen Helene she'd been about fourteen or fifteen.

"When did it happen?"

"Not quite three weeks ago."

"Then what the hell are you doing here? Why aren't you in Indigo?"

Her arms wrapped across her stomach, she clutched her sides as if to hide her skin, her self. "Because this is where she was living. This is where she died."

"The police are sure?"

"That she's dead, yes. That she was brutally murdered, yes. That they have few leads. Yes! The invitation was the only lead I had!"

"You have to let the police handle this."

She looked at him. "Would you, Hunter? Would you if it was Temple or Logan or Nash? Would you just sit and wait?"

"I'm not you, Eden. You don't have the means, the experience."

"She's my sister! The police didn't find Helene's ex-roommate, or her things or that invitation, Hunter. I'd hired a private investigator."

"I want his name and all the information."

"Where do you get off making demands to me?"

"I told you—"

"Nothing, Hunter, you've told me nothing. And if you want information, Nash was the officer on the scene. He has the official files. Call him." At the mention of his police detective brother, Hunter's features shuttered closed. It was a very telling look. His family would be furious to learn he was in the U.S. without coming to see them, or calling. "I'd hired a private detective *before* she was found murdered. Helene had cut me out of her life months ago, refusing calls, refusing my help, and when I learned she was on a steel slab with a white sheet up to her throat, I learned why."

His expression questioned.

"She'd had a baby."

His features pulled taut. "Recently?"

"Yes. Only a day or two before her death, the coroner said. The baby is missing and I need to find her, or him. I can't stay here and exchange barbs with you. It was a mistake to come here." She headed to the door. "I have to go back to the party. It's the only clue I had."

Hunter cut her off, grasping her arms and wrestling with her for a second. Then she gave up. "Eden, look at me." She lifted her gaze and Hunter saw the sheen of tears, but she wouldn't cry. He didn't know how he knew it, but she wouldn't let him see her cry. "If I swear to find the baby, will you go home?"

She blinked. "That's a big promise, Hunter. And what makes you think you can?"

"I won't stop looking."

"Neither will I."

A growl rumbled in his throat before he said, "God, you're still so stubborn." He let her go, turning away and rubbing the back of his neck. If Helene had been killed for her baby, like the others, then why didn't the FBI know about it? Local law-enforcement departments didn't readily share information unless asked, and the FBI was more than likely trying to keep quiet till they could get someone inside. It pissed him off.

"If you go back to the ball and start asking questions, you're putting yourself in danger."

"My life. My risk."

"I won't allow it. If I have to arrest you, I will."

"On what grounds? By whose authority?"

"Eden."

She folded her arms across her bare middle and marked time by tapping her foot on the carpet. "Show me a badge or I'm gone, Hunter."

Sighing, he went to his briefcase, opened it, then

flipped the billfold out so she could read it. Her gaze focused on the ID, then flashed to his eyes.

"You're kidding."

"What? It doesn't look real?" He glanced at it, then stuffed it inside his jacket again.

"CIA? Do you think I'm stupid?" She shook her head. "CIA doesn't have jurisdiction in domestic matters. So what would the CIA be doing on a murder case in South Carolina?"

Hunter knew she wouldn't leave unless he convinced her he could do as he promised and find Helene's baby. Without a word, he moved to the wet bar, selecting bottles and glasses. "I want your oath, Eden."

"I swear. Now what am I swearing to?"

"Not to reveal what I tell you," he tossed over his right shoulder, then poured.

"I swear."

"Good. Sit down and let's talk. The party is nearly over by now, anyway."

Eden accepted that if she left now, it would be winding down by the time she returned to the plantation. She moved back to the window, tossing her handbag and cloak onto an overstuffed chair. She crossed her arms over her bare stomach and gripped her elbows, watching the city lights glitter and seeing only her sister, fighting for her life. And losing.

"It was my one good chance."

"There's always another."

Except with him, she thought. She could barely

look at him right now. Then Hunter moved up beside her, handing her a small draught of almond liqueur in a crystal goblet.

She took it, and tossed it back in one gulp. It burned smoothly all the way down, chasing the chill. At his look, she sent him a tight smile, then said, "Convince me why I should go home."

"Three women have been murdered, four, counting Helene. All having recently delivered a baby. But there's no trace of the infants."

Her eyes widened as he spoke. "Oh, my God. Do the police have leads? Do they have any idea what happened to the babies? Why new mothers? Is it a serial killer?"

She went still and swallowed, her heart racing a mile a second and her mind reeling. She dropped onto the sofa. "Someone is killing women for their babies."

"Yes." He went back to the bar and refilled her glass, bringing it back to her.

She started to drink, then just clutched it tightly. "Tell me the truth. You owe me that much."

"I've said enough and the less you know…"

"The safer I will be?" She popped off the couch. "Do you think I care? I've already lost my parents, and now my sister. Helene's baby is the only family I have in the world, Hunter. So you have a choice…you either clue me in to what you know or I'm outta here. I'll take my chances at what's left of the party." Her eyes narrowed. "Or you'll be tripping over me in this investigation."

The changes in her blasted him in the face. So much more fire and attitude. And it was sexy as hell. Feminine power. The woman he'd left years ago wouldn't have bucked against him or anyone before. She would have been a peacemaker, and have accepted instead of fought. Now she wasn't accepting a thing, including him.

"Well?"

He sighed. "I stumbled on a black-market baby ring, purely by accident, in Istanbul." Working a female slavery case had brought him to the tender cargo being transported to Europe. Babies, brought in with fake parents, fake passports. The anger still burned inside him.

"What were you doing in Turkey?" He eyed her and she sighed and said, "Okay, I won't go there."

"We've managed to find four babies illegally adopted." Her face lit up and her hope made him ache inside. "But that was in Europe. After interrogating those involved, I suspected there were more and the trail led me here. The mothers were all young, destitute and murdered."

"So what are you doing about it here?"

"Hunting for the leader of the ring."

"Are you succeeding?"

"I just got here a few days ago, Eden, and I was making progress till you walked into that ballroom."

"You came to me," she reminded. "You could have stayed in the background, Hunter. Steered clear of me. I wouldn't have noticed you."

She was right. He'd moved on instinct when he'd seen her, felt the need to connect to her. "But I noticed you, and so did the other men, and now that I know you were asking questions, I'm glad you're not there. Asking questions would have put the dealers on your trail and you in danger. Missing, murdered, pregnant women isn't common conversation, and we don't want to alert them. They've killed to keep this quiet, Eden, and we don't know how many seemingly random deaths are connected."

A ringing sound came from his pocket and he pulled out a cell and moved away to take the call. His tone was hushed, yet Eden heard the timbre of authority. He ended the call without saying goodbye.

"Come on." He picked up her handbag and cloak. "You need to come with me."

"Where now?"

"The FBI will want to talk with you." And he wasn't letting her out of his sight till he was certain she'd go home.

"The feds and the CIA? Oh this really deserves an explanation."

Hunter almost smiled, sweeping her cloak over her bare shoulders and wondering when the battle lines would be drawn again.

IN A SUITE in the Regions building, the FBI resident agency offices weren't anything impressive. What was, was the way the agents treated Hunter. With barely suppressed animosity and respect. Special

Agent in Charge Aidan Crew ushered her into a room and questioned her politely. Hunter stood in the corner, arms folded, and said nothing. Crew, a not-too-shabby-looking dark-haired man probably in his mid-thirties, ignored Hunter. Eden figured it was a territorial thing and she waited for one of them to mark their corner.

"Helene sounded fine, happy when I talked to her last, which was about a month and a half ago." She looked from one man to the other. "It was a shock since I hadn't heard from her for about four months. I couldn't convince her to come home to visit, but then, I thought she was in college, getting her degree."

"She wasn't?" inquired Crew.

"She hadn't been in class for six months. Her things were gone from her dorm except for a box my private investigator found." Eden opened her evening bag and slid the card across the table. The agent glanced at it, then handed the card to Hunter.

"Hope Randell?" Hunter said. "I thought she was a cop."

"Not for a few years now. She does some bounty work, too."

Hunter tossed the card onto the table, shifting his position.

"Did Helene give you any indication that she was pregnant?" Crew asked.

"No." Bitter hurt spun up to choke her. It was tough to admit to strangers that her sister had cut her out of her life. "We used to be close, but Helene always did what she wanted. She was impulsive."

"You aren't impulsive?"

She kept her gaze on Crew. "No. I was responsible for her since our parents died."

"This isn't about Miss Carlyle," Hunter interjected tersely.

Crew looked at Hunter briefly, then back to Eden. "Did she have a boyfriend? Or give you any indication who the father of her child was?"

"She mentioned some guy named Harry less than a year ago. But in our last conversation she didn't mention him, so I assumed the relationship was over."

Hunter stiffened. "You didn't tell me that."

She lifted her gaze to him. "You didn't ask." She sipped coffee from a foam cup. "I imagine this is all in the police report, Agent Crew."

"We're waiting for it. Did your sister mention going to a free clinic?"

Eden frowned. "No, why?"

"We've traced the only other common factor of the last victims to a free clinic. We questioned everyone and finally learned a worker there was passing information to the conspirators. He told them when there was a young unwed mother coming to the clinic."

"My God. That's like pointing out a woman to be killed!"

"I agree, ma'am. He contacted the dealers by pay phone, but their number changed each time. It would be in a letter slid under his apartment door."

"So this worker doesn't know anything?"

"Not enough." Crew studied her for a moment. "What did you hope to accomplish at the charity ball?"

"Get a name, maybe an idea of why my sister was invited."

"And what would you do with it?"

"Give it to the police, of course." Eden opened her beaded handbag, and slid the invitation toward Crew. Hunter's gaze thinned and Eden gave him a bland look.

Crew glanced between the couple, then asked, "What did your sister say about Harry?"

"That she was in love with him and he was great, but Helene went through men, Agent Crew. I love— loved—my sister, but I knew what she was like. She lived for the moment and did what pleased her. She's had her share of trouble a couple times with the law when she was a kid. Going to college was the longest she'd stayed with any task. But when it came to men, it didn't take much to make her walk over one and go on to the next."

"You don't think this Harry was the father of her child?"

"Possibly, but I also think that if Helene believed he wouldn't agree to have the baby, she'd never tell him the truth. Or she'd just vanish to avoid facing it."

Crew sighed.

"As well as I knew my sister, Agent Crew, I don't know why she would have been invited to that party, or why she would have kept her pregnancy from me.

Except that she still saw me as a mother. She was fourteen when our parents died."

Crew nodded and stood, gathering papers and taking the invitation.

"I'm not much help, am I?"

His sympathetic gaze touched hers briefly. "More than you think, ma'am. I'll send someone in to take a record of your statement."

Eden looked at Hunter. "What now?"

"Just sit tight." Hunter followed Crew.

Eden muttered, "Only for now, Hunter. For now."

HUNTER AND CREW moved to a room just to the right, the two-way glass unnecessary, but it was the only private spot tonight. Hunter stared through the glass at Eden.

"Well, so much for your expertise as a spy."

Hunter glanced at Crew. "Look into David Winston and a Paulette and Chase Ramsgate. They were chatting about adoption to another couple."

"Ramsgate will be easy. He's all over this state. Senatorial aspirations." Crew jotted down the names. "But why Winston?"

"He doesn't know Eden's name, but he was flirting with her."

"And this means what, Couviyon? Other than jealousy?"

Hunter shot him a hard look. "I don't know who else noticed her or talked to her. Did you think to ask that?"

"Did you?"

"She's not exactly forthcoming with me."

Crew leaned back in the chair, tapping the pen for a second. "How well do you know her?"

"Very well."

"Apparently you're not on her best-date list."

Hunter rolled around, his back to the glass, his gaze landing on Crew like a hammer. "I was engaged to her seven years ago. I broke it off."

Crew leaned forward and looked at Eden, then back at Hunter. "Now I *know* you're not as smart as we all thought."

Hunter scowled.

"Nothing like a woman scorned."

Hunter shook his head. "Eden wouldn't do anything to jeopardize our work. She wants to find that baby as much as we do."

Crew's gaze kept shifting to Eden. It had been the same since they'd walked in. Just about every male agent here had popped out of his office to get a look at her. Especially with her belly showing in that low-riding gown—did designers go out of their way to make men crazy with dresses like that?

"Order her home," Hunter said.

"She's a private citizen."

"She's involved. She's related to the victim and has a stake in the capture. And she's already tried investigating on her own." The thought of Eden putting herself in danger pumped up his blood pressure. "She's been seen already." He gestured to Eden, looking exquisite at midnight.

"Are you certain no one saw you two together except Winston?"

"No. We danced. It was the only way to get her…secured at the moment. But she'd chatted with people and she was already there when I arrived."

Crew tossed his pen onto the files. "That blows it for the undercover work we'd planned."

"Not really. If anyone asks, she's an old friend. We go as planned with Sanders." Agent Sanders was the woman who was to pose as Hunter's wife. Together they would make contacts to buy a baby.

"Miss Carlyle makes it sticky."

"I know."

"We have to do something about local, small town departments not sharing information ASAP. We should have been on her sister's case three weeks ago."

Three weeks meant the trail was growing cold. "Let's get on it. Tonight," Hunter said. "Shake some people awake, and start the setup for the sting."

A knock came, a second later an agent came in, looking upset and holding a slip of paper. "Marcia, ah, Agent Sanders is in the hospital."

Both men cursed. "How?" Crew said, reaching for the paper.

"Bank robbery. She took a bullet in the stomach just below her vest. But she's going to be fine. In a few weeks."

Hunter opened his jacket and shoved his hands into his pants pocket. Agent Marcia Sanders had been briefed and was ready, but she'd asked Hunter to postpone the first stage because she'd been working on a serial robbery case and she was close to tying it up. He'd allowed it because he'd understood her need to take it to the end, yet it had almost killed her.

Crew instructed that an agent be posted at her hospital room and Hunter laid a twenty on the table for the flowers they'd send.

"It's not hopeless, we get another agent." Hunter's brain scrambled for ideas.

"Do you know how few available women agents there are?" Crew said. "Ones who know the area and could pull off acting like they were born to money and privilege?"

Hunter looked down at Sander's file picture. She was attractive, in her late twenties, and he would have pretended to love her enough to lay out a million in cash for a baby. Now they were back to square one, and Hunter wondered if he could con the director into finding him a CIA operative to fit the bill. Not much chance of that. Strings had been pulled to put him here already.

"There is one other option we haven't considered," Crew said.

Hunter looked up, frowning, his gaze shooting between Crew and where he was looking. At Eden.

Chapter Three

"Are you insane?" Hunter demanded. "Eden Carlyle is a civilian."

"I don't like this idea, either. But the groundwork has already been laid. People saw you dance and saw you leave with her. That puts *her* face in the right place, with *you*."

Beneath his anger, Hunter admitted that major screwup was his fault. "I'm not risking her life. She's not trained, for God's sake. She's a…she's…" Hell, he didn't even know what she did for a living. It didn't matter. He was not going to spend the next few weeks locked in mortal combat with Eden.

"She won't have to do more than put in appearances, dangle on your arm to get these people to show themselves."

Hunter's pale eyes narrowed. It was more than that and they both knew it. They'd have to behave as husband and wife 24/7. It had to look real. "You don't send civilians into the battle, Crew."

"Listen, Couviyon, this is my investigation as

much as yours. We've asked civilians for assistance before. Eden has been estranged from her sister for months, and from what Eden said, Helene didn't share personal information so there's a good chance the perpetrators don't know what she looks like. We have a serial killer cutting the throats of young, helpless mothers. We don't have time to get another agent. You've already put out feelers and a wife *has* to make an appearance in days." Crew stood, moving to the window, looking at Eden. "And you've been seen together," he reminded needlessly. "And likely seen leaving together."

Crew was right. A wife had to appear, Hunter'd dropped subtle hints all week. But his personal feelings were involved, and that he was allowing them to matter made him feel as if he wasn't giving a hundred percent to the job.

"Would she play the role?"

"That's debatable." Especially when she heard the plan.

"But is she capable?"

Hunter looked at Eden, saw her smile at the female agent as she answered questions. Seven years ago, she wouldn't have had the guts to do what Crew was asking, but she was so different. She had drive and a strong will now, and while Hunter wouldn't admit how much she excited him, he knew the truth. "If you asked, she'd think she owed her sister and that makes it dangerous. She walks in with a big stake in it. The question is, will I allow it? No."

Crew gave him an arch look. "I thought CIA did what it took, no matter who got crushed."

Hunter turned his head, his eyes glacial. Crew shifted where he stood. "Yeah, that's right."

He didn't get to be a CIA attack dog without letting some blood. But this time, it was Eden. And no matter how much she loathed him, using her would be like leading a lamb into a pasture populated with hungry wolves.

"What's bothering you more, Couviyon? The fact that she won't or that she just might agree?"

Hunter pushed away from the wall. "Find someone else." He left the door swinging behind him, striding down the hall toward the break room, ignoring the looks. He wasn't a familiar face, he was CIA, after all, but standing in a tuxedo in an FBI regional office at midnight was enough to bring stares. In the break room, he grabbed the coffeepot and poured.

Crew was crazy. The setup had to look real, and pretending to be married, eating together, dressing, bathing and sleeping in the same room would be agony. For both of them. He'd have to face more than Eden. He'd have to face the reasons why he'd left and that chewed at his gut more than Crew's outrageous ideas.

But Hunter wanted the killer; he was sadistically itching to get his hands on the perps and make them suffer for their crimes. He wanted strong, unquestionable evidence. Coming face to face with the people perpetrating the black-market baby operation was the only way. The FBI had barely scratched the surface after three murders. Now there was Helene, and Alice Crane could be number five.

Pushing aside his anger, he looked at the options objectively, with opportunities, scenarios and possible dangers. If he kept Eden close, she'd be safe. If he gave up this chance, the whole operation could go down in one conversation between the right people.

They *had* been seen and Eden had been right, it was his fault. He'd gone to her. The ballroom had been crowded and if he'd just stayed back, they might not have met again at all. That would have been the end of it. He'd screwed it up. But Crew was asking Eden to fix his mistakes.

Could he ask her to risk her life with him, when he knew good and well she would never trust him again?

He swilled bad coffee, wishing it was something stronger, and realized with some shock that he was shaking a little.

HELENE CARLYLE'S police file arrived by e-mail attachment, and Crew was in the hall, thumbing through the printout when Hunter walked up behind him.

"She got it worse than the others," Crew said sadly. "Drugs in her system weren't as much as the other victims, but she has the markings of our killer. Except she fought him." He handed it over, and Hunter read as he stepped into the interrogation room.

Eden yawned, her hand over her mouth. "Sorry," she said as Crew handed her a fresh cup of coffee.

"Get the forensic DNA on the victim," Hunter said to Crew, still flipping through the report. "I want them at Medical University of South Carolina lab in case we get something to match it against. We'll have to move fast. Go through the victim's college records, question professors, students."

"Agent Yudell looks young enough to still fit the college crowd," Crew said. "That'll shave down some resistance."

Hunter nodded, though he didn't know the agent. They all looked a little too fresh-faced to him. CIA never worked domestic crimes. Hunter was in this because he found the black-market ring and was ordered to follow it to the end.

"The victim worked at a sports bar part-time, too." Crew gestured to the report. "But her driver's license was expired so she must have taken buses or walked."

"Or driven illegally," Hunter said. "We need the victim's belongings and to question the P.I., Hope Randell. She'll have turned anything she found on the victim over to the police, but I doubt it's made it into a report yet."

"Stop calling her that!"

Hunter looked at Eden.

"Stop calling her the victim." Eden stood, her gaze pinning Hunter. "She was Helene, Helene Marie Carlyle." She took a step closer to Hunter.

"She played with Barbies till she was twelve, and she could draw like nobody's business. She stuck a potato in your tailpipe, remember? Your precious '65 Mustang wouldn't run for a week." His tender look said he remembered. "She showed up at my college graduation looking like something from Guns 'N' Roses. She'd have sworn up and down that nothing would get to her, but she still cried when she left home for the first time. She was a person." Eden fought the sting of tears. "My baby sister! She wasn't a victim. That killer *made* her his victim!"

"Sorry, Miss Carlyle," Crew said, a little red around the ears.

"Me, too, Eden," Hunter said, his expression gentle for the first time tonight. He laid the report on the gray desk, but when she reached for it, he covered her hand. "No. You don't need to see those."

"Oh, Hunter, no one should see a twenty-two-year-old woman with her throat cut and her face battered."

It was far worse than that and Hunter pulled the file back, refusing her a look at the crime-scene photos. Yet he couldn't take his gaze from hers, her soulful green eyes looking for some small gesture that he'd find Helene's killer and make this right for her.

Eden lowered her gaze. "I'm tired, I need to go home."

"Good. I'll have an agent ready to drive you to Indigo," Hunter said.

Her head snapped up, her gaze thin. "I have a car, and I meant my hotel. I'm staying."

"Like hell. You'll go home where it's safe."

"Save the bullying for the criminals, Hunter. I'm doing what I have to do, so forget about looking all official and barking orders." She folded her arms, her eyes flashing with impatience. "You don't scare me."

Hunter assumed the same position. They stared each other down.

"Miss Carlyle," Crew spoke up. "You've walked into an investigation and since clearly you aren't going to give up your hunt for the killer, we are obligated to put you under protective custody."

She looked at Crew. "As in, lock me up till it's over?"

"Yes, ma'am."

"And you'd allow that?" she said to Hunter.

He could see the hurt in her eyes. "Yes. If you interfere, it not only puts your life in danger, but also mine and the other agents on this case."

"I can't go where you can, and besides, you're trained for that sort of stuff."

Hunter looked pointedly at Crew as if to say, *See what I mean?* "What do you think you can do, Eden?"

"I don't know, but what are you going to do that the police haven't?"

"We'll get inside the ring."

"How?"

"We were contracting for a baby."

Her breath skipped. "Were?"

Noise outside the room escalated and sent Crew

to the door. "Guess they heard." He opened it, demanding quiet, then turned back.

"Sounds like the posse gathering," Hunter said.

"Yeah, but the shooter's behind bars already, so they're all ready to go after his accomplices."

"Someone was shot?" Eden's gaze moved between the two men.

"One of our agents took a bullet tonight, ma'am."

"Oh, no. Is he going to be all right?"

"It's a woman, and yes, thank you for asking." Crew's gaze flicked to Hunter's. "But it puts us in a bad predicament. Since she was scheduled to start an undercover assignment."

"Crew," Hunter warned.

Agent Crew looked at him. "Couviyon, we need her."

"Who?" Her eyes rounded, her gaze darting between the men. "Me? You're kidding."

"Yes, he is." Hunter glared at Crew.

"Do we have a choice?" Crew replied crisply. "She's not leaving and I don't want to lock her up. Do you?"

"How about we see if anyone remembered her and then go from there."

"Good God, look at her. She's hard to miss."

Hunter knew exactly what she looked like. Sexy, exotic, with a bared navel that gave him ideas of some slow tongue dipping and on to softer places below her tan line. He tried not to think about it. Much.

"Was that a compliment? Because if it was, thanks."

They didn't hear her, facing off like two bulls in a pen.

"And if we ask about her, it will only bring more attention. Agreed?"

Hunter hated to admit it, yet nodded.

"Stop talking around me, it's rude." They looked at her, blinking for a second. "And if you need me to find the bastard that killed my sister, just ask. I'll do whatever it takes, follow any orders." She looked at Hunter. "Including yours."

Hunter looked a little miffed, but Eden didn't care. She needed to do something and while working with the FBI sounded exciting, she understood the danger.

Crew's smile went slowly wider.

"What do you need from me?"

"To portray his wife," Crew said, tossing a thumb at Hunter.

Eden blinked. "Oh." She swung her gaze to Hunter, trying to read his expression and failing to pierce that icy stare. "A husband? That ought to be a tough role for you."

"This is strictly business."

"I never assumed otherwise."

She said it with such dignity, with complete aplomb that Hunter experienced a jab somewhere around his heart.

"Let me explain the situation before you agree."

"That's not really necessary, Agent Crew. I'm aware of what portraying a wife entails. Make it look real, live together. Behaving in a loving manner?"

Crew nodded.

"And I'm sure Officer Couviyon has told you that I'd agreed to be his wife several years ago." Her gaze slid to Hunter's.

"Then do it again," Hunter said, knowing it was hopeless to fight the situation. "Be my wife, Eden." The soul dropped out of her heart, as it had when he'd said those words once before. Then he added, "Help me catch a killer."

THE FBI WENT INTO ACTION. The setup was elaborate and took two days. The timber magnate and his wife emerged in fake marriage licenses, titles of homes, bank accounts and with the advance of technology, computer-generated photos were fabricated. There were pictures of Hunter and Eden at social functions, holidays, weddings, all stuffed in the archives of newspapers. The FBI techs inserted Eden's photo in the places prearranged for Sanders. SLED, South Carolina's State Law Enforcement Division, was in on the sting, keeping the murders from making the paper and following clues that only officers who'd lived in the area all their lives could find. They owed a lot to SLED.

Hunter switched his accommodations to the historic Mill's House Hotel, and into a suite that offered more rooms and romantic privacy. He didn't let himself think about living there with her. He just did what he had to do.

The FBI laid out funds for limousines with undercover agents as chauffeurs and the suite's closets were filled with tailored suits and casual clothing for him, and triple the amount of outfits for Eden, with shoes and bags and whatever else she'd need filling dressers and closets. She brought her own things anyway, telling him that wearing panties that every FBI agent had seen or selected was way beyond the call of duty.

It was strange seeing his own clothes next to hers, and Hunter tried not to dwell on it. They had a job to do, and though this was the ultimate payback for leaving her, Hunter would do everything he could to get Helene's baby back. He prayed the child hadn't been whisked out of the country by now.

In addition to the clothes, cars and room, jewelry was also purchased. It looked like half of the Harry Winston collection was in the wooden jewelry case on Eden's dresser, and when Hunter came to Eden in the hotel room, he gripped the wedding rings they were to wear.

He handed her the box. She frowned at it first, then looked up. He showed her his hand, flicking the gold and diamond band.

"Oh. I hadn't thought of that."

She opened the box and inhaled at the almost garish set. "This is not me."

"So? It's supposed to scream money, Eden."

"Well it does, but it should be my taste, don't you think?"

"No. It's a damn ring. Put it on." Hunter did not want to have this conversation.

Irritated with his callousness, she stood, leaving the ring on the sofa.

He watched her walk toward the bedroom, then scooped it up. "Eden. Put it on. You agreed to take orders from me if you were going to work on this case."

"Fine. But I'll only wear it in public."

He caught her, slapping the velvet box into her hand. "What's your problem? It's not a real marriage."

She shoved it back. "Gee, I'm so stupid I forgot all about the FBI surveillance team across the street, the taps on the phones, and thought, wow, I'm miraculously married." She scoffed. "What do you take me for?"

His gaze softened a bit. "Someone who's still mad at me after seven years."

Her eyes turned glacial. "Mad? I'm not mad, Hunter. I got over being mad and hurt a long, long time ago."

"Then what's the deal?"

Were all men really this dense? "How about a real explanation?" She folded her arms and cocked her head. "An apology for humiliating me in front of the entire town, your family? And leaving me alone to clean up the mess!"

"What mess?"

Her heart broke again, the little pieces jabbing through her bloodstream. "The mess that had people saying I wasn't good enough for you. The one that had everyone giving me sympathy and chastising you, yet no one could look me in the eye without thinking 'oh poor pitiful Eden, that's what she gets for trying to snag a Couviyon.'"

"And you believed that bunk?"

"Think about it, Hunter. Shy, poor girl wins the heart of the richest playboy in South Carolina, and then, just weeks before they walk down the aisle, he says, sorry, can't do this and vanishes. What did you expect to happen to me? Or did you even care?"

"Of course I cared. I loved you."

The arrow shot straight into her heart and made it bleed. "No, Hunter, you didn't. Or you would have asked me to join you." Tears frosted her eyes.

"And you would you have gone globe-hopping with me?"

"That's sort of a moot point now, isn't it? I'm glad we didn't marry."

His features tightened sharply. "Oh, yeah?"

"If you could choose being double-oh-seven over me, what else would take you so easily from me?"

She turned into the bedroom and quietly shut the door. No slamming, no tears, no shouts, just silence. Hunter felt as he had seven years ago, when he'd broken their engagement. She'd shed a couple of tears, nodded, then simply handed him back his ring and turned away.

It was as if she'd expected him to let her down and had just accepted it. A guy couldn't have asked for a smoother breakup. But just looking at her now was killing him inside. Because she might claim she'd gotten over him, but being near her the past forty-eight hours, Hunter knew, he'd never gotten over her. He'd just ignored it.

And for the next weeks, it was going to take everything he had to keep that wall up.

Chapter Four

This first night in the suite was murder.

The luxurious accommodations paled compared to seeing Eden in a silk nightgown and robe. The damn thing clung to her body like a second skin and sent his pulse climbing a couple of notches.

She paused at the bathroom door, meeting his gaze, then moved quickly to the side of the bed.

"Do you prefer a certain side?" she asked softly, then snapped a look at him, her cheeks flamed.

She knew exactly how he'd slept, at least she had years ago. Now it was more with one eye open than in a restful slumber.

Shaking his head, he shrugged out of his jacket and hung it up. He didn't want to remember how it felt to lie in her arms. For years he'd suppressed the memory. But if she didn't get her sweet behind under the covers he was going to do something stupid like flatten her on that bed and reacquaint himself with his past.

Damn. He turned, weakened by the sight of her

sitting on the bed. He strode across the room, thinking that all the resistance training in the world wasn't helping him now.

Eden glanced at him as he passed close, then forced her attention elsewhere. It landed on the pair of wedding rings nestled in the velvet box. She'd meant what she'd said about not wearing the ring unless it was playing the role. She already had too much of a reminder that they were pretending the marriage they should have had seven years ago.

They were no more than two strangers in the same room, each with high stakes in solving this crime. Eden's stake was more personal, and she knew she was merely useful, a pawn in the game. If she hadn't been, she'd be under lock and key at home. Her gaze followed Hunter as he moved to the dresser.

Hunter could feel her watching him, and it made him uncomfortable as he plucked at his cuff links, tossing them onto his dresser. The dresser opposite his was decorated with the jewelry box and an array of glass bottles. Even the maid had to believe they were married and swimming in cash. Gossip was going to be their best weapon in some instances. As Hunter kicked his shoes into the closet, Eden pulled back the spread, then slipped off her robe.

He caught a whiff of her perfume, and his gaze snapped to her, traveling over the waterfall of hair shining in the lamplight. His fingers practically itched to dive into it and he busied himself with turning back his cuffs. But the gown was cut deep in the back, showing him the intoxicating curve of her spine before she slid under the sheets.

He had to get out of here. Immediately. Hunter went for his laptop hidden in the room safe and punched the combination.

"You look exhausted, Hunter. What could you possibly learn at this hour?" she said.

Hunter removed the case, struggling with the image of her in that thin gown in that big king-size bed—without him. "I have files to study."

"Will you keep me informed or am I just going to be expensive window dressing?"

He met her gaze as he stood. "I'll let you know what I have. We just don't talk about it in public where we might be overheard."

"I know. Agent Crew warned me."

She'd been briefed on how to handle this, that the slightest thing could alert the wrong people. Eden understood that outside these walls she had to pretend to be in love with Hunter, that she was Mrs. Hunter Lockwood, wife to a timber magnate.

Wondering what his older brother Logan would say to that, considering he was the real timber tycoon in the family, Hunter said good-night and was about to close the door behind him, when he paused in the doorway.

"Thank you for doing this, Eden." It couldn't be any easier on her, he thought.

She blinked, a little shocked. "I have a stake in finding the killer, too, Hunter. When we do, we will find Helene's baby."

He hated to break her heart, but… "The chances aren't good, you have to know that up front. The birth was three weeks ago. The ring I uncovered in Istanbul had month-old babies. Helene's child could be out of the country by now."

Eden's heart sank a little. "I know, but I have to hope. That child is all the family I have left."

"I find it hard to believe you don't have someone waiting for you in Indigo."

Eden's brows rose. "What makes you think I don't?"

"Do you? I don't want some civilian coming in here unannounced." Half of him wanted her to be engaged, married, anything to make her off-limits. The other hoped she'd be free, though he knew he didn't deserve a chance.

"No one but Hope and your brother Nash know I'm here," she said evasively.

His gaze narrowed. That didn't mean a man couldn't come looking for her.

"I have a business to get back to soon, regardless."

"What will you do about your business till then?" He frowned. "What is it anyway?"

"I own a café on the waterfront, Eden's Rest."

He whistled softly. A waterfront business in a seaside village? "Bet that rakes in the cash."

"It's popular with the tourists. Very relaxed. It's done well enough that I'm not hurting." Eden adjusted the sheets, not wanting to discuss her private life with him. It had taken two jobs and every penny she had to buy that café. "I have a manager who can handle it well enough, but I'll have to check in with her. I'll have paychecks to sign, too." She frowned, wondering how she was going to handle that. The accountant would do the paychecks, but they had to have her signature. She hadn't planned on not returning home and if she expressed them overnight, she'd have to reveal her real name. At least she had two weeks till she had to be concerned with that. "It's the start of the off season, so business will slow down for a month or so."

He nodded, his gaze moving over her with such intensity, Eden slid deeper under the covers. "Good night."

Feeling dismissed, Hunter closed the door, and let wisdom seep into his brain. Sleep on the sofa, not the bed. He couldn't get that close to Eden. Even if he wanted to.

IN THE MORNING, room service delivered breakfast and coffee, and when Eden came out of the bedroom, Hunter was already enjoying his first cup. The delicate china looked like a toy in his big hands, and she felt his gaze on her as she moved to the sideboard and poured some for herself.

"What did you find?" She nodded at the laptop. "Have you been up all night?" His clothes were rumpled.

"No, I slept on the sofa."

"The bed is big enough, Hunter, there's no reason for that."

As far as he was concerned, no bed with her in it was big enough. "I had to work." He reread the screen, then looked at her.

"Okay, so tell me what you've learned that I didn't hear from the FBI."

Hunter waited till she was seated before he picked up his fork. Eden mused that his polished breeding hadn't worn off that much in the past seven years. His mother would be proud of him.

"The murders were made to look like suicides. Three so far. Except Helene's." He flipped open the laptop and turned it toward her.

Eden buttered her toast, stretching in the chair to read the file. "What's the difference?"

"She fought her attacker. And that gives us DNA evidence." Eden looked confused. "Under her fingernails. The coroner believes she scratched him."

"Excellent."

Hunter's lips curved. "Unlike the other three girls Helene didn't have much drugs in her system, which is likely how she managed to escape."

"Escaped from where?"

"We don't know, but I think the pregnant girls are being held somewhere. Their children are taken at birth, and then they are murdered and dumped with nothing to lead anyone to the black-market ring. I need to find that location."

"You think there are more pregnant women being held?"

"No reason not to. They've gotten away with this

so far, and I found American babies in Greece, Turkey and France."

"How'd they do that? Babies have to have passports, right?"

"They had forged papers and passports."

Eden eyed him as he devoured eggs, bacon, toast, fried potatoes and grits in short order. She'd forgotten what it took to keep a big man fueled. She scrolled down the file.

"If there are women being held, do you have any missing-person reports that would match up?"

He shook his head. "I have no proof anyone is being held. It's a theory. I think they prey on women who don't have anyone or who they think don't have family. Like the ones at the free clinic. Senator Crane's daughter, Alice, is a runaway and we think—"

"Who? What are you talking about?"

"I'm on this with the FBI because I found the slave trail, then the baby ring trail in Europe and it led me here. And because the senator's daughter is missing. She was pregnant and ran away, last seen around Charleston."

"You think this girl is a hostage?"

"I'm hoping. If she isn't, she's dead. Senator Crane was a fraternity brother. Needless to say, he pulled some strings to get me here when he'd learned the details from the director. Since I can't walk the streets, SLED and local police are looking for Alice during this operation." He drained his coffee. "I'm going to shower and change. We need to start this thing out there." He inclined his head toward the windows.

She nodded. "What do we do first?"

"We meet with an adoption lawyer, make appointments with a couple more, then let it be known in casual conversation that we're here to adopt. A lot of locals come to this hotel and people always ask what tourists are doing in their city."

"Good thing I don't leave Indigo much then. I'll look like a tourist. I haven't been to Charleston in a year."

Her gaze snagged on his, remembering when they'd taken a trip here. He'd showered her with attention and they'd stayed in a bed and breakfast on the Battery.

"How about a tour of the city then?"

"That's not getting us the killer," she said, not wanting to be anywhere romantic with him. She was the means to the end, someone who'd make this all appear believable. She had gone past believing there was a chance for them years ago.

When he didn't come back.

When he didn't call, write, e-mail.

"We have dinner reservations in the Barbados Room downstairs."

He left the room, and a few moments later she heard the shower. Eden closed her eyes, wishing away the memory of Hunter, naked. But it came. Dark wet hair, soap foaming over all that muscle.

Like his brothers, he was a towering man, big shoulders, wide hands. She shifted in her chair, stuffing a piece of toast in her mouth.

No woman should have to live with the man she'd loved, knowing he'd never love her in return again.

HUNTER WINCED when the door of the lawyer's office slammed behind him.

Eden fought a smile. He was scowling at the door.

"So would you consider being shoved out the door a mark of success?" Eden said as they walked to the limousine at the curb.

The FBI driver opened the door.

"I'd say he's on the up and up."

Eden ducked into the limousine and, tucked in the corner, she smiled as he settled in. "Did you see how fast he ushered us out when we mentioned paying any cost?"

"I think it was the implication that we'd be willing to pay to skirt the usual requirements that did it."

"I thought he was going to shove us down the staircase," Eden said.

"I bet he's telling his secretary to burn the paperwork as we speak," Hunter said. "That will get talk going though. They meet and eat in the same places."

"Doesn't this feel like a waste of time and people?" Eden said, taking out her lipstick and compact.

"No, this is a sting operation," Hunter explained, watching her. "The more like real candidates we are, the better our chances are of getting the leaders and the people who have killed."

Eden looked at her lap.

"What?"

She lifted her gaze. "I find it hard to believe that anyone would kill a young mother for her child."

"I don't."

She arched a brow.

"I've seen people killed for less. For no reason."

Before she could ask more, Hunter pulled out his cell phone, hitting speed dial. "You get all that?" he said to Agent Crew and Eden frowned at him. "Yeah, it's working fine on this end." Hunter showed Eden the wire inside his jacket. The mike was hidden in the handkerchief in his breast pocket. "No, I don't want her wired." His attention slipped to Eden as she freshened her lipstick. "It will show." Eden's silky dark-pink tank top and matching skirt were thin and too clingy to hide a wire. But damn if she didn't look like a perfect little rose in the corner of the limo seat, her matching bag on her lap, ankles crossed. Her hair was braided in a twist with soft curls dancing on a neck he wanted to nibble.

Hunter hung up.

"Why don't you want me to wear a wire? I can hide it well, I think," she said looking down at her breasts. When she lifted her gaze, he was staring at them.

His gaze snapped to hers. "No. The nicer the rack the more some idiot will try to cop a feel."

"My, how nicely put."

She wrapped her arms across her middle and looked out the window. He knew she was irritated now.

"What's the problem?"

"I think you're letting your personal feelings get in the way," she said.

"I don't want you to get hurt."

"And with you next to me twenty-four hours a day, how could anyone touch me?"

Hunter gnashed his teeth, wanting to do some in-depth touching himself. "Hence, no need for the wire."

The car pulled up along the Mill's House on Meeting Street and Hunter left it first, turning back for her. He held out his hand, giving her a tug and she shot out of the car and landed in his arms. She stared up at him, her body pressed to his and the shock of it left them both pulsing for more.

"Smile, people are watching," he said.

She slid her hand up his lapel and curled her fingers in his hair. "What would you like me to do, Hunter?" she said in the sexiest voice he'd ever heard.

His gaze raked her face. "Kiss me."

"Is this for show?"

"Not really." Before she could move, he leaned, drawing his arms tightly around her and laying his mouth over hers, kissed her deeply enough to let everyone who was watching know they'd been intimate, that they'd loved.

Which wasn't too hard.

Eden sank into him, tightening her fingers in his hair as he took control, his warm tongue slicking the line of her lips, then dipping inside.

Someone cleared their throat and they parted slowly.

Neither smiled, both breathing hard. Hunter eased his hold on her, and didn't glance at the agent posing as the driver as his hand slid down her arm to grasp her fingers.

"Good enough for show?"

"Hum?" Eden was numb. Every inch of her felt languid and aroused. Their kiss had been different than before. Heavy. Like a fine wine, he'd aged well and so had his kissing.

Hunter pushed a strand of hair off Eden's face, breathing hard.

The doorman was grinning.

"Fine, I'm fine," she muttered, and warned her feet that not walking in a straight line right now wouldn't be good for appearances. They obeyed.

Hunter pressed a hand to the small of her back as they passed into the foyer, and the smack of cool air pushed away the haze Hunter left around her. She looked at him, wondering if he felt anything but duty, and absently reached to wipe away the lipstick on his mouth. He caught her hand, holding it for a second.

What was going on in his mind, she wondered, because all she saw when she looked up at him was cool blue eyes without a shred of emotion. Telling him she'd meet him in the Barbados Room, she excused herself and hurried in to the ladies' room. Safe inside, she sighed against the wall.

Oh, this was not good, she thought, still feeling the imprint of his body against hers. She practically hummed with capped energy. This is a game, he feels nothing, she repeated in her mind. She'd have to avoid kissing him. It wasn't necessary, right?

A noise stirred her out of her thoughts, and she recognized the sounds of a baby. Her heart tumbled and when a woman came out of a stall with a child, Eden couldn't help but stare.

The woman was smartly dressed, the child wrapped in designer garments and blankets. "What a pretty little girl," she said. The child couldn't be more than a month old.

"She's my pride and joy," the woman said, adjusting the frilly bonnet.

"Would you like some help?" Eden offered as the woman struggled to wash her hands with the child in her arms.

She gave Eden a look that told her she was sizing her up.

"Yes, thank you." She handed the baby to her, and Eden cuddled the little girl close. "They should have changing counters in here. Funny that you never think of that till you have a child."

"She's beautiful." A lump worked to a knot in Eden's throat.

"She's my second."

"Really," Eden said, putting envy in her voice that was all too real.

"We adopted her."

Eden lifted her gaze, hope in her eyes. "That's why we're here. My husband and I just went to an appointment with a lawyer about private adoptions. We've been on a list for years and I'm tired of waiting."

The women dried her hands, then fished in her handbag for a business card. "This is the lawyer who handled Cecilia's adoption."

Eden took the card, then handed the child back.

"It was expensive."

Eden waved that off. "That's not the problem, it's finding a child and a lawyer who will handle it privately. And quickly."

"She will." The woman nodded to the card. "She doesn't advertise, either."

"Why not?"

"I don't think she wants thousands of couples coming to her when there aren't enough babies to offer."

Eden clutched the card. "Thank you so much. I can't wait to tell my husband."

The woman smiled down at her child and Eden's heart rolled in her chest as the infant drew a deep breath and sighed in her sleep. Was there anything in this world more beautiful?

The woman left and Eden used the facilities, then hurried into the dining room.

Hunter stood as she neared, holding out her chair. "Eden," he began softly. "About that kiss…"

Seated, she tipped her head back and whispered, "It was a kiss for show, Hunter, I know." Though he always could melt her stockings. "I have something that might help us."

He slid into his chair, frowning.

She offered the card. "A lawyer who does costly private adoptions but doesn't advertise."

"This is fantastic. How did you get that?" he said, reaching for it.

"You'd be amazed at the things you can learn in a ladies' room."

Hunter stared at the card, then met Eden's gaze.

Her smile lit up the room, her eyes dancing with the thrill of success. Seeing it hit him square in the chest, and something sprang to life inside him.

He shouldn't be thinking about anything but the case, the murders, but a hundred thoughts and old memories trotted through his brain just then. The day he'd walked away from her. He didn't deserve a second chance. Besides, his job kept him from pursuing it. But the one thing he could do was work hard to put her last living relative in her arms. To give her something before he disappeared from her life again.

He looked down at the card. If this paid off, they'd be ahead of the game. One step closer to nabbing the monsters who'd brutally murdered her sister.

Chapter Five

"If I wanted to be on a list," Hunter said tersely. "I'd be in a state agency, not here."

"Darling," Eden said, laying her hand on his arm. He looked at her, his lips tight with feigned frustration.

"You knew all the money in the world wasn't going to move this any faster, right? We discussed this."

Eden looked at attorney Roxanne Mitchell seated on the other side of the wide polished desk. "Forgive his impatience, Miss Mitchell. Hunter's used to getting what he wants when he demands it." She sent Hunter an endearing smile.

Hunter admitted she was good. Really good. If he wasn't careful, his heart would start believing the act they were playing.

"I understand, believe me," Mitchell said, leaning forward and folding her manicured hands on her desk.

In a pale-gray suit, Roxanne Mitchell had *shark*

written all over her, Hunter thought, from the severe twist of her hair, to the heels that could kill a man if used correctly. Hunter wasn't impressed, and without meaning to, he compared Eden to this woman.

Eden was curvy and immersed in femininity. Mitchell seemed intent on keeping it at bay.

"The process takes time," Mitchell said. "Mothers aren't running to put their babies up for adoption as much as they were even five months ago."

"I'm willing to pay anything to hurry it up," Hunter said.

"Hunter," Eden scolded gently. "You're not giving Miss Mitchell a very good impression."

He met her gaze, shifting toward her, and touched her cheek in a way that was somehow more intimate than anything they'd shared before.

"I want to be able to play with our child, Eden, and not from a damn wheelchair."

Eden smiled, her heart in her eyes. At least, she hoped it was, as she turned to look at the attorney. Roxanne Mitchell returned her stare without a shred of emotion. She wasn't biting, Eden realized, her disappointment real.

"We can't have any children of our own, and we've exhausted fertility treatments."

"The drugs were too much for her and I nearly lost her," Hunter said, sticking with the plan the FBI had implanted in records and documents. For emphasis, he brought her hand to his lips and kissed her knuckles. Then he turned sharp eyes on Mitchell. "If you can't help us, then we'll find someone who's better equipped to do it."

Hunter stood abruptly, pulling Eden from the chair. They moved toward the door.

"Mr. Lockwood," Mitchell said quickly. "I'll look into it for you, but you must be willing to wait it out."

"We're not going anywhere."

Hunter pulled out his checkbook and wrote a check before she could protest. "This is to retain your services, and put a little fire under it."

"Hunter," Eden said, appalled.

He glanced between the two women. "As my wife said, I'm not good at waiting." Hunter slid the check across the desk. "Good day, Miss Mitchell."

He escorted Eden out, then, just beyond the front doors on the street, he pulled her into his arms.

"Hunter?"

"Act as though you're upset," he whispered.

"I am upset. You were downright rude."

"We want her to think this is traumatic. Cry."

Eden bowed her head and did a little choking, covering her mouth, shaking her head. Hunter ducked to look at her face, rubbed her arms, pretending to soothe her. Then suddenly she threw herself into his arms, and buried her face in his neck.

"How's that?"

For a moment he savored the feel of her body laid against his. "Great, great," he said, rubbing her back. Over her shoulder, he looked for a distraction. "Here's the car." Thank God.

Eden stepped back, fishing in her handbag for a tissue for added effect.

The black four-door sedan pulled up and the driver hopped out, frowning. Hunter waved him back and helped Eden into the car. Inside the car, he looked through the black tinted glass up at the old building, and caught a glimpse of Mitchell moving away from the window.

He sat back. "She was there, watching."

Eden's brows shot up. "How'd you know?"

He shrugged, then spoke into the mike in his lapel. "We have a fish on the line."

Eden wasn't so convinced. "Did you see how quickly she snatched that check and read the amount?"

"But she wasn't angered by the implication, nor was she shoving us out like the last one. She didn't follow us out the door, either. Normally she would have."

"You think she was waiting for a reaction from us?"

"Oh, yeah," Hunter said. "Let's hope it worked." He leaned back in the cushions, his gaze on Eden. "You were great, you should have been an actress."

Her smile was thin. "I want this bad enough that I'm willing to do most anything to find Helene's baby."

Including live with him for weeks, he thought, but wasn't opening that door.

"What's next?"

"We wait. If she'll contact us, then we should know something in twenty-four hours. If not, I'll call her and push her along."

"Perhaps I should?"

"I don't think so."

"I do. You were abrupt and arrogant. I was level-headed. She'll talk to me more easily."

"You would never have done anything like this seven years ago," he stated suddenly.

"I wouldn't have done a lot of things then, though I was forced to."

"Raising Helene must have been difficult."

A loving smile laced with regret shaped her lips. "She was a handful, and worse for her was that I didn't know how to raise a fifteen-year-old. I'd always behaved, did what I should. Helene was never predictable."

"And you were."

"That sounds very close to an insult, Hunter. You remember a doormat? A wuss?"

He scowled. "I didn't mean it like that and you know it."

"Do I? Seven years ago I thought I understood you." The car stopped. The doorman of the Mill's House opened the passenger door immediately. Eden slid to the edge of the seat, then met Hunter's gaze directly. They were nearly nose to nose. "But not anymore."

She left the car, walking to the covered entrance and waiting for him as he paused to speak to the driver. Despite every vow not to let her feelings for him surface, when he walked toward her, her heart skipped a beat, then pounded furiously. He swept his arm around her, drawing her inside, and Eden reminded herself that this was for show. She meant nothing to him but a reminder of his past, a past he'd hated enough to leave her without ever looking back.

THREE HOURS LATER Eden swept into the hotel suite and dropped the half-dozen shopping bags on the bed. "I never thought I'd ever say this, but I'm shopped out. Done."

"You'll have to keep it up this week, and if all pans out with Mitchell, it will be baby things you'll shop for next."

Eden blinked. "Okay, that I won't mind, but there's something about buying things with money that isn't yours for things you won't be keeping that feels like stealing."

Hunter looked confused for a second then said, "Pretend."

"I am, I was good." She waved at the bags from the finest shops in Charleston.

"Good? How about the jewelry store?· Oh, Hunter," he mimicked. "The necklace is too much, I don't need it."

Her hands on her hips, she stared at him, not at all amused. "No woman needs a ten-carat diamond necklace, Hunter. Borrowed for this operation or not."

She might be spoiling for an argument now, but the candid awe in her expression this afternoon still played in his mind. Though it had delighted him to see it, it wasn't part of the game. "See, you're thinking practical."

"I *am* practical."

"Well think rich, dammit."

"Easy for you to say, I've never had the silver spoon in my mouth."

"You'd be surprised at the high price that comes with that spoon," Hunter muttered just before his cell phone rang.

It was a satellite secured line, he'd told her, and when he listened to the caller and scowled, she couldn't tell if it was good or bad. Hunter did a lot of scowling anyway.

"If she's clean then she's clean," Hunter said into the phone.

"I didn't say that," Agent Crew said on the other end of the line. "She's clean, on the surface. She's handled several private adoptions. She was on our list, so I have some preliminary information for you. I'm sending it e-mail now."

Hunter moved to the safe, removing his laptop and opening the lid. Eden made no attempt to understand the high-tech equipment Hunter had with him. Listening devices, microphone bugs, body wires that were as small as his cuff links or that fitted inside a seam. His computer was satellite-linked and he didn't even need a phone connection. She was living with James Bond, she thought, and peered over his shoulder as information ticked across the screen. He glanced back at her, frowning.

"National secrets?"

"No, but if you want to read it, sit. Not over my shoulder."

He'd been testy for the last couple hours, but then shopping will do that to a man.

He muttered something to Agent Crew, then hung up and focused on the screen. Eden felt instantly shut out. If he thought that stony silence would work on her, he was wrong. She sat down beside him, picking up papers and glancing over them.

"So, explain how you've come up with this." There were sheets of note-filled paper scattered around the table.

"These are other possibilities. I have to consider that there might be another motive."

"Such as?"

"A serial killer."

"Isn't that what we have? Someone who's killing for babies? Acting out some twisted fantasy? I bet a psychologist will tell you the babies are trophies." Even as she said it, she paled, misery racing through her and burning her eyes. "Oh, Hunter, what if—"

"Don't. Don't think that way, not yet." He closed his hand over hers on the table. "I've found a child in Europe, Eden, alive. But we have to be methodical and turn each clue over and over." She nodded and he let her go, looking at his work. ViCAP, Violent Crime Apprehension Program, had a database and agents working around the clock. Information on Helene's murder has just made it into the computer, Crew had told him. "The profilers say our killer is between twenty-four and forty-five." She made a face.

"Meticulous, considers the kills personal because all were with a knife. He wants the bodies to be found or he wouldn't have chosen shallow graves. He's not killing the women where he leaves them."

"Do you know where he's killing them?"

He shook his head.

"So he's transporting the dead women?" She shivered at the thought.

"This guy leaves behind nothing to trace him with. No hair, prints, saliva, semen, zip. Any DNA we have has to have a source to compare it with. So we focus on the victims and commonality. Aside from the fact that the murders are made to look like suicide, except Helene, the victims had red hair, again except for Helene. Hers was dyed brown."

"That's conservative for her. She tinted it ten different shades in a year. Pink, blond, green once. But it was naturally red, lighter than mine though."

Hunter didn't have to confirm it in the report. He'd known Helene. "All were college age or younger. Not all were from Southern states. But each was alone with little money and no family contact within the last seven months. Except Helene. Two of the four had families searching. You, and now Senator Crane."

"The other girls, no one filed a report on them?"

"No."

"If your theory is right, they kidnapped them and hid them some place till they gave birth. What did the guy at the clinic say?"

"He was contacted by phone, paid in cash through a post-office box, no trace. The number he called to give information changed each time."

"Can't you see what calls were made to that pay phone, trace them backwards?"

"Yes, but the calls were routed through another blind phone line."

"I don't understand."

"A call is placed, but instead of a direct phone line, it's hopped through servers in different countries or states, through a computer. The caller would have been at a computer, talking into a microphone and you'd hear it through a phone."

Hunter turned the screen toward her and tapped a few keys. She saw a dialing read out, then watched a map of the world appear. A blue line jumped across the screen from South Carolina to England to Crete and a half-dozen other places before coming back to South Carolina.

The phone rang in the room and Eden blinked and reached for it. "Hello."

Hunter slipped on a head set and said, "See."

"Oh, that's amazing!" she said, hanging up. "How can you track a phone call with that kind of stuff?"

"The more technology we have, the harder it is. Teenagers can do this easier than I can."

"Helene was a whiz at computers, art graphics mostly." Eden inhaled briskly. "Did they find her laptop? I got her one before she went off to college."

"They didn't even find her ID, Eden," Hunter said. "Indigo police identified her from fingerprints."

Any hope Eden had dissolved. "She'd been hauled in for drag racing. In my car." She smiled at the memory. "I had to put new tires on the car, plus bail her out of jail. But since she was underage, her sentence was cleaning up the highway and no driver's license for a year."

"She really was a handful, wasn't she?"

"Oh, yes," Eden said dramatically. "She was so angry after our parents died." And personally hurt when Hunter left, but she didn't mention that. "Even before that, she rebelled against any restrictions."

Hunter recalled Helene the first time he'd taken Eden out. Helene had leaned against the doorframe, popping gum and giving him the once-over, before saying, "You think you're good enough for my sister, rich boy?"

He hadn't been, Hunter thought, and looking at Eden now, he knew that for certain.

Abruptly, Eden left the chair and moved to the window, staring out at the cobbled street. "I guess I should have been stricter with her. Maybe then she'd be here now."

"Eden, don't beat yourself up over it. She was a grown woman."

"No, she wanted to *be* grown up, Hunter. But she didn't even have the chance to learn who she really was." She bowed her head, and she choked on a sob, covering her mouth. Hunter was behind her, his hands a gentle weight on her shoulders.

He didn't know what to say, how to soothe. Her world had come down to just her, alone, and a missing baby.

"I'll find the child," he said.

Eden turned, tipping her face up, and Hunter felt pierced to his soul by those glossy green eyes. "I know the odds, Hunter. Please, don't make any more promises you can't keep."

DAMPNESS SEEPED, sweating the walls, the unending silence broken by the frantic pulse of a heartbeat. It was a valuable sound. Almost like the chink of coins. Under dim light, they lay in a neat row, plump and motionless, monitors tracking the life growing inside them without their help. Without anyone missing them.

The mounds rippled with movement.

He wasn't awed by the sight.

They were machines. Nothing more than profitable mechanisms spitting out a product. One twitched and his attention narrowed on the flexing fingers.

Pretty manicured fingers, he thought, touching the healing scratches on his clean-shaven face. He'd liked the last one. The redhead, wild and outspoken.

A fighter.

Killing Helene had been a battle and the memory of it hardened his groin. He fought the urge to ease it, clenching his fists. But denial intensified the need.

Instead, he adjusted his tie, tugged at his silk cuffs, then walked nearer. One stirred, but he knew she couldn't see him clearly. His gaze shifted to the IV, and he reached, increasing the dosage.

Her body went soft, her belly shifting.

Hurry up, he thought, crushing the urge to cut the baby out of her.

Chapter Six

Eden was driving him insane.

With hunger.

With want.

He wanted to see her smile at him and not behave as if she was a lamb in the lion's den.

She'd played the role in public, hanging on his every word, on his arm, but in the suite she was cool and spoke little. For two nights, she'd curled up on the corner of the huge bed like a rabbit.

Hunter slept on the sofa and his mood was paying for it.

The fictitious Lockwoods had millions, all electronic, and twenty-four hours ago they'd learned someone had accessed their financial records. Roxanne Mitchell. No surprise there. The fact that she was the Ramsgates' attorney and that they had a new privately adopted baby was a piece of the puzzle. A weak piece, because private adoptions weren't illegal.

While the FBI was eager to take Mitchell in, they

couldn't move till the sting was over. Mitchell was under surveillance around the clock. Hunter had spent the last two days rereading every piece of information he could get and knew he needed more, something that would take them in a new direction. He hoped it wasn't another body.

Anything, he thought, so he wouldn't be occupied with watching Eden. She was a walking temptation, moving around him as if he wasn't there, her perfume and the rustle of silky clothing enticing him. She could do the most trivial things and he'd be turned on. Hunter faced the fact that Eden could do that with just a smile. Always could. And having her this close yet this untouchable was turning him into a shell of the trained operative he once was.

When she flitted in and out of the room for the tenth time, he snapped, "Will you just sit!"

Eden stopped short, unaffected. "I'm not used to doing nothing."

"But even the maid has to think that you've done nothing." He nodded to the towels in her arms.

She laid them aside. "All right then, give me something to do. By now I've opened up my café and the morning rush of customers would already be out the door."

Hunter opened his mouth to utter a sharp retort when the phone rang in the hotel suite, the sound snapping at the tension between them.

Hunter moved toward it, letting it ring once more before picking it up. "Hunter Lockwood."

"Mr. Lockwood," an unfamiliar voice said.

"Miss Mitchell?" Hunter motioned Eden near and they listened together.

"Oh, no, dear. But I'd like to speak with you in person."

"Make an appointment with my secretary."

Eden's eyes flared at his rudeness, but Hunter had already built a reputation, and he had to stick to it.

"I was under the impression you wanted help."

"With what?"

"Expanding your family."

Hunter's gaze snapped to Eden. She was practically wringing her hands. "And where did you hear that?"

"Is that really important, Mr. Lockwood?"

The caller gave an address and time. Hunter jotted it down.

"Can I expect you?" the woman asked, her voice sounding older than Mitchell's.

"Tell me what this is for?"

"An interview."

"Yes, we will be there."

"Alone."

The line went dead. Hunter hung up and hurried to the satellite phone, dialing Crew.

"Did you get a trace?" Hunter asked, knowing the hotel lines were tapped.

"Not yet," Crew said. "It isn't a star-sixty-nine thing, you know."

"I'd bet it's a blind line, like the kid from the clinic."

"We've got people searching out the address." Crew was quiet for a moment, then said, "It's near Mount Pleasant. You don't have much time to get through traffic."

Hunter hung up and looked at Eden, her eager expression whittling at his composure. He was bringing her into danger now.

"Get ready, we meet with them in two hours."

"Oh, my God."

"Wear something that screams rich, Eden. And jewelry." He grasped her hand, arching a brow at the fact that she wasn't wearing the fake wedding rings.

"It will have to be subtle, tasteful," she said, pulling free and heading to the closet as Hunter went to the bathroom to shave.

An hour later, Hunter was behind the wheel of a slick black sports car, headed to the address. Eden's stomach was in knots that tightened harder with each mile.

"If you were really looking for a baby to adopt like this," he asked, "what would you ask for?"

"Red hair like mine. Blue eyes like yours. Good Lord." She looked at him, horrified. "It sounds like a shopping list."

He reached over, patting her hand. "The business of selling babies is ugly," he said.

The car phone rang. "I'm getting sick of that thing," she said and answered it.

"The owner of the property is Margaret Harker," Crew said. "We don't have a photo yet."

She relayed the information to Hunter. "We're already here, Aidan."

Hunter pulled the car into the driveway of a two-story Charleston-style house, and Eden handed over the car phone.

"I'm in a car a mile behind you," Aidan said to Hunter. "We'll circle to the back street behind the house."

"Roger that," Hunter said. "We don't want to scare her and if she's as cautious as we think, she'll smell you coming."

Hunter hung up, left the car, then moved around to Eden's door and helped her out. He stared down at her, forcing her to meet his gaze.

"Are you ready for this?"

Eden nodded.

"Just be yourself, Eden, and you'll be fine."

Hunter pressed his lips to her top of her head. Then he eased back, taking a breath, then grasped her hand.

They walked up the flower-lined sidewalk and onto the porch that ran along the length of the house. He rang the bell and looked down at Eden, admiring her bravery. She was the picture of sophistication in a slim-fitting black skirt and dark-beige buttonless jacket trimmed in black braiding. Beneath it, the scooped blouse showed off the black pearl necklace that was worth more than the car they'd arrived in. Sophisticated and lovely.

She was something else, he thought, feeling the

burn of pride as he gazed down at her. She looked up, smiling nervously at him.

That was the picture Margaret Harker saw when she opened the door.

Hunter turned his head and hid his shock. She looked like his grandmother. Petite and silver-haired, Margaret Harker had the slump of age in her shoulders, and a road map of creases in her face. Dark eyes twinkled as she looked from one to the other.

"We're the Lockwoods."

"Of course you are. Come in."

She stepped back and Eden proceeded in, her hand still clasped in Hunter's.

"Why don't we go into the parlor?" the woman invited, then led the way.

Hunter scanned the room in one sweep, noticing exits and windows, the doors leading elsewhere, then the piano, the lack of dust and the careful arrangement of so much bric-a-brac he thought he'd knock something over.

The woman gestured to the dainty settee and Eden sat, tugging Hunter down beside her as their hostess got comfortable in the chair opposite. There was a silver tea service on the coffee table between them.

"How did you learn of us?"

"I listen to gossip, and I heard about your problem."

Eden looked at her lap.

The woman must have thought it was embarrassment, and said, "Now dear, lots of women can't have children. But that doesn't mean they shouldn't have babies to raise."

Eden looked up, hopeful.

"Would you like some tea?" the grandmotherly figure said, smiling, her apple-cheeked face glowing with warmth.

Eden nodded. "Who are you?" she asked.

"Oh, dear, forgive me, I'm Margaret." She poured two cups, offering one to each of them.

Hunter didn't decline, but he wasn't drinking anything this lady prepared. Especially when she wasn't joining them.

"You have a lovely home, ma'am," Eden said. "Is that a Steinway piano?"

"Yes, it's been in my family for years."

"I love the painting over the hearth."

The women chatted about gardening and flowers, antiques and the aged photos hung on the walls. Hunter listened, sizing up Harker and the situation. The room might looked lived in, but he got the feeling it was more for show. Not a thing was out of place; it was all too carefully arranged.

"You're a very handsome couple."

"That's all due to my wife," Hunter said quickly.

Margaret smiled benignly. "Why don't you tell me how you met?"

Eden glanced at Hunter, gripping the edge of the saucer so the woman wouldn't see her shaking. "I'm afraid I hit him with my car."

Margaret blinked, then grinned, showing perfect

false teeth. "Well, this sounds interesting," she said. "Tell me about it."

Hunter looked at Eden as she told the story of how they'd really met. Her brakes were sluggish, he'd been stepping off the curb and she'd hit him. A light tap, but enough to knock him over. She'd rushed from the car, kneeling on the pavement in her skirt and stockings, cradling his head in her lap, and crying.

"I stared up into those soft green eyes and was lost," he put in.

Eden looked at him, her heart pounding as she sank into his gaze.

"I didn't want her to leave so I made a show of being injured."

"I didn't care if he was faking," Eden said, "I thought he was the most handsome man I'd ever seen and I'd nearly killed him."

"She was in tears, panicking, but she wouldn't leave to call for help. Not that I needed it," he said with a wink at Harker. "I'd taken harder hits playing football."

"He teased me, asking if he'd hurt me in another life and was I trying to pay him back?"

Their expression grew somber, the similarities of then and now hitting home.

"And when did you know you loved her?" Margaret said, looking between the two.

Hunter cleared his throat. Eden looked at her teacup, her face flaming.

"I'm sorry for being so personal, but really, I need to understand you and your relationship."

Before she can select us as candidates, Hunter thought.

Hunter looked at Eden, his mind clarifying memories he'd shelved and never drawn out to examine. "It was a hot summer night, really still. Where you sweat just because you're breathing. We were by the river."

"Oh, Hunter, don't," Eden said as that night flooded back.

"I knew I loved her when I complained about the heat and she said she knew how to cool off. She stripped down to her skin and dove in the river."

"Hunter!" Eden's cheeks burned.

"I knew then she was a strong woman with her own mind." She could have withstood the scrutiny that came with a being a Couviyon, Hunter thought. "It was something else because she'd been the shy girl," he said, warming to the subject. "Hiding behind all that hair, and in my opinion, skirts that were too long and not showing me those legs."

Eden looked at Hunter as if he was crazy, fighting a smile.

"And Eden, how about you?"

She didn't take her gaze off him when she said, "I loved him even when I was sleeping."

Hunter's expression tightened, the sting of regret lancing through him.

"I didn't care who he was, his money, his family,

nothing. Only him. Only the chance to love *him*." Her eyes burned and she looked at Margaret. "When he proposed, he'd made me believe in dreams and happy endings again."

And he'd destroyed them by leaving, Hunter thought, the punch of her words hitting dead center in his heart.

Margaret glanced adoringly between them and Hunter slid his arm around Eden, pressing his lips to her temple, knowing she was hurting inside. And he was the cause.

"Well, I see that you're very much in love. Is there room for a child?"

"Yes," they said in unison.

"I'd wanted to give Hunter a child, but it wasn't meant to be," Eden said, bowing her head as old memories lashed at her composure.

"Perhaps we can change that," Margaret said cryptically. "Can I assume you're looking for a redhead?" The woman leaned, fingering a lock of Eden's hair and she had to force herself not to cringe. No matter how kind and motherly she seemed, this woman had, quite possibly, helped kidnap and murder her sister.

"Yes, we are," Hunter answered, squeezing Eden close and disengaging Harker's touch.

"The sex?"

"It doesn't matter."

The woman stood, and Hunter took the signal to mean the interview was over. They walked to the door. He noticed the stairs to the second floor, and the door probably leading to the kitchen. The good thing about Charleston-style homes was that the floor plans were usually the same in all of them. The land was at sea level so there wasn't a basement, he thought, noticing there wasn't another sound in the house aside from their footsteps. Not even the hum of a refrigerator.

At the door, Hunter faced Margaret, all pretense vanishing. "I'm willing to do anything to give my wife those dreams again," he said. "We want a child, a newborn, and I have the money to make it happen."

"Hunter! Must you be so blunt?"

He looked down at her, touching her chin in that way that made her whole body jump with anticipation.

"Don't you know, darlin', I'd do anything just to see you happy?"

Eden's lip trembled. She kept telling herself it was a game, that Hunter was playing the same role as she was. Yet when she gazed into his blue eyes, she remembered—for one small second—exactly how deeply she'd loved this man.

She smiled. They said goodbye and, tucked close to each other, they went to the car. In moments they were driving away.

Hunter checked in the rearview mirror, noticing Harker looking around before she backed into the house and closed the door. They drove past Crew sitting in a parked car hidden beneath gnarled oak trees dripping with Spanish moss.

"I hope they got all that."

When Eden didn't respond, Hunter looked over at her. She had a tissue crumpled in her hand and he saw a single tear plop onto her clenched fist.

"Eden?" He swerved to the side and threw the car into Park. "What's the matter? You were great in there."

"I can't do this." She shook her head. "I can't."

"I'm sorry you had to relive that, but we tell the lies to get close to the source."

Oh, that was cold, Eden thought, meeting his gaze. Because they weren't all lies. "No, we did it to get a baby…my sisters or another's. But if Harker finds us a child that means an innocent woman will lose her baby and possibly her life!"

"This is the only way we can get them. It has to be this way."

She stared into unfeeling eyes. Eyes that had shown great tenderness only moments ago. "How can you turn it off and on like that?"

"It's my job."

"Doesn't it bother you that while you're all con-tracting for a child some young mother is out there being stalked? They will kidnap her, scare her, then take the only thing that's giving her hope?"

"Of course it bothers me! Dammit, I'm not made of stone. I want to kill the bastards who hurt these women. No," he corrected, "I want to torture them. But if I work from my emotions I won't find the killer or the babies. The person who is murdering these women sure as hell isn't letting anything stop him."

"I know that! But all I can envision is Helene being snatched and terrified out of her mind."

Hunter's expression softened with understanding, knowing her active mind was torturing her. "So can I, Eden. I knew her, too."

Eden didn't know that Helene had been chased, hunted in the woods like an animal. Weak, alone, without her baby, Helene had tried to fight off her attacker. Then the bastard had cut her throat and buried her while she was still alive. Hunter would do anything to keep those details from Eden.

He gripped the steering wheel, wanting his hands around the bastard's throat. He wanted vengeance for the young girl who had lived life with a chip on her shoulder. And he was going to get it.

Angrily, he pulled into traffic, barking at Crew to back off.

HE BENT AND SLAPPED her face, waiting till she focused on his. He knew the instant she understood.

Terror bloomed.

He smiled.

She tried to move and couldn't. He didn't need a fight this time. The drugs had seen to that.

"You did very well, my sweet."

Another man snickered nearby, turning his face away to light a cigarette.

"No," he said, and the younger man dropped it,

grinding it under his boot. "Pick it up, leave nothing behind."

He looked back at the girl, smiling tenderly.

He had a prize from her, a million dollars' worth of wriggling flesh and blood. Now she was useless. And he had to clean up his mess.

With meticulous patience, he unbuttoned his jacket, folding it lining out and laying it on a fallen tree. His gaze shifted to the young punk, and he inclined his head. The kid moved away.

He finished stripping out of his clothing, down to his bare, shaved body. His hands were sealed in gloves, his feet inside plastic. He lifted the girl from the truck, cradling her in his arms like a child, and carried her into the woods. She didn't have the strength to fight him. Yet in slurred murmurs, she begged for her life. For her child.

He ignored it.

Her contribution was done. And it belonged to him.

He laid her on the forest floor, arranged her limbs. He'd leave nothing behind. He'd considered burning her, but the smell would alert others.

She tried to move, to crawl away.

He squatted beside her, taking her hand in his. "It won't hurt for long."

Her eyes widened. Her mouth opened, yet sound failed.

"It's your fault. You can't keep a child when you're turning tricks." Her confused fear didn't penetrate his mind. "I'm saving him."

He twisted to reach the knife buried in the ground, letting her see the curved razor point of black steel.

His groin throbbed as her panic multiplied. His erection grew.

Grabbing her wrist, he turned the blade handle toward her, then drew it across her wrist. The cut was to the bone. Blood curtained and he held her fingers for a moment, smearing it on her palms and fingers, then letting it flow, disguise. He moved to the other side, and sliced open the other, making certain the drag was weaker, that the right-handed cut was stronger.

He dropped her hand as if it offended him and rose, stepping back. He watched her face, the plea in her eyes as the blood drained from her body with the pump of her heart. His erection throbbed, yet he was still, watching her till her breathing stopped, till the soft gurgle spilled.

Then he covered his tracks, stirring the matted ground as he backed toward his clothes. At the fallen log, he dressed slowly, taking time to affix the gold collar stay, to precisely tie his calfskin shoes.

The punk appeared. The man inclined his head and the kid went for the body.

He'd left nothing behind—nothing that was his.

THE EVENING had an edge on it.

The air in the spacious suite was cold and banked with a thickness that weighed on them both. They'd dined in the room. The danger Hunter had put Eden in, the worry that something could go wrong tightened his spine till he had a headache the size of a cannon blasting behind his eyes.

They snapped at each other to the point that Eden marched off to bed.

He checked the locks, the windows, then ordered the surveillance crew to back off. He'd allowed phone taps and clothing wires, but inside the hotel room, they were cocooned in the plush hotel, alone, with no distractions but each other.

Hunter poured two fingers of Scotch in a short tumbler and tossed it back in one swallow. The burn of it in his stomach spread like a fire as he tried blocking the image of Eden's distraught face from his mind, the crime scene photos of Helene, her throat split open, her body covered with dirt.

He gripped the tumbler, considered a second drink, then set it aside and walked into the bedroom. Eden was asleep, the book she'd been reading on her stomach. He moved quietly, pulling the book free and turning off the light on the bedside table. Then he noticed she'd turned down the other side of the bed for him. Ignoring it, he stripped out of his clothes and slipped on a pair of cotton drawstring slacks.

For a moment, he simply stared at her.

I loved him even when I was sleeping. It echoed in his mind, and the ache in his chest magnified.

Hunter eased onto the bed, reaching, needing to touch her skin. He didn't; instead, he sanded strands of her hair between his fingers, wanting to lock her in his arms and forget about the past, about the pain he'd caused her.

But there was no use even in dreaming of it.

She didn't trust him, and he doubted she ever would.

He didn't blame her one bit.

He wasn't sticking around after this. His theatre of work was eastern Europe and he needed to get back to it. He needed to make certain the line of baby sellers was severed.

Easing back on the pillows, he watched her sleep, finding a crumb of peace to know that she was near.

In seconds, he was asleep.

Within minutes, he was trapped in Somalia—again.

EDEN STIRRED, hearing a strange noise. Fear slipped over her in a cold chill, and carefully she moved to her side, looking around the darkened room and wondering what had woken her. Then it came again and she sat up, staring at the shadowy mound beside her.

Hunter.

Moonlight barely touched him as he shifted in his sleep, mumbling to himself, and when he slammed his fist onto the mattress she flinched and realized he was caught in a nightmare. He cursed and struggled, gripping the covers so tightly she heard his knuckles crack.

She couldn't understand what he was saying, it

was slurred and in a language she didn't recognize. But she felt the frustration and anger in him. Rage contorted his handsome features into something scary, someone lethal.

Wondering if she'd accidentally get belted in the process, she rubbed his shoulder as she whispered, "Hunter? Wake up. It's a nightmare."

He grabbed her by the arm, his grip punishing. "You die tonight!" he snarled.

"Ow. Hunter! Wake up." She shoved hard. He pulled her till she was in his face, murmuring a threat to tear her apart. My God, what kind of life had he been leading before now? Fighting panic, she forced herself to relax and whispered his name, talking of gentler times and trying to pull him back to reality.

Gradually his grip softened and she found herself clamped against his broad chest, his thick arms imprisoning her. Eden kept stroking his face, his shoulder and when his breathing slowed, Eden rested her cheek on his chest, a tear spilling for the man he once was and the one he'd become.

She held him, feeling oddly safe. When he whispered her name in his sleep, she smiled, following him into calm dreams.

Chapter Seven

Wrapped in her dreams, Eden felt warm, a gentle stirring coiling through her. His mouth traveled over her throat, nipping, licking, and she tipped her head back, offering more as his hand swept down her spine and under her nightgown. The warmth of his palms seeped into her skin, relaxing her in her dream, making her feel boneless and cherished.

Then his mouth covered hers, soft at first, then plundering, a heated, eating kiss that curled her toes and made her reach for him, pull him closer. His broad palm swallowed her bare breast, fingers circling her nipple till it peaked and tightened. Melting her insides.

She drank it in, feeling as if she'd waited a decade to feel his hands on her again. She moaned, liking this dream, wanting more, and when his touch moved down her body, she arched into it. Opened for him.

His hand dove smoothly between her legs, driving desire and anticipation up her limbs. She was liquid soft and without willpower and let the dream take her somewhere erotic and lush. He rubbed gently, and her breathing increased, her kiss growing hungrier as she shifted into his touch. He kissed her as though he wanted to draw her inside him, devouring and hot, his tongue licking the line of her lips, prying them open, then slipping inside.

A moan pierced the silence and she knew it was hers, knew that she could let loose in the dream. He pulled her to the edge of hunger, parting her delicate flesh and slipping a single finger smoothly inside. She gasped at the delicious invasion, instinctively thrusting to it, and while he never ceased kissing her, he manipulated her body like a fine-tuned instrument.

He always could. Hunter was the only man who could sense her mood and make love to her the way she needed. Slow and sweet, or fast and fiery.

His touch slickened her, her muscles humming with energy waiting to be uncapped. When she touched his face and opened her eyes, she realized it wasn't a dream.

He stared down at her, his expression tight with his own need.

"Hunter."

His lips quirked. "Who'd you think it was?"

"I—I thought I was dreaming."

"So did I."

"Well, stop." She grabbed his arm.

He shook his head. "You're on the edge, Eden, I can feel it. Some things I never forgot."

He moved his hand back and forth, thrusting in

the way he wanted to be pushing inside her. He circled the bead of her sex and her breath skipped as
she tried to fill her lungs.

He knew she was near.

"We can't. I don't want this."

"You sure?" He introduced another finger and
pushed deeper, her body flexing.

"Oh, Hunter." She dragged it out, moaned it.

He smiled, a tender, loving smile she hadn't seen
in years and her resolve vanished. She plowed her
hand into his hair and pulled him close to kiss him.

"Damn you."

"I know, I know, baby," Hunter said and quick-
ened his pace, his arousal rock-hard and ready to
slide inside her, feel her pulse around him.

But he wouldn't. He'd been dreaming, too, and he
should have stopped when he'd woken enough to
know she was really in his arms, and responding to
him. He'd resisted torture for ten days, but Eden,
naked and panting, was his greatest weakness. And
right now, he didn't want to resist her.

He pressed her to her back, nudging her thighs
apart and fairly imprisoning her on the bed. He met
her gaze, lowering his mouth to the sweet tip of her
breast and closing his lips around her nipple. He
drew it into his mouth and she arched, a silken rib-
bon of beauty beneath him.

"Hunter," she cried in the dark, holding him
closer. Her hand glided down his body to the band
of his cotton pants and he stopped her.

"No, I won't complicate this more than it is."

"But—"

"I'm being noble, take it."

He drove deeper, obliterating any thoughts and taking her toward the brink of rapture. He leaned over her, his expression possessive as he watched her face, wanting full light to see her quiver as she climaxed.

Then she did, thrashing on the pillows, her body in command, and when he swept his thumb around the sensitive nub, she gripped his arms and gasped for air.

"Over, let yourself go over," he whispered.

Eden cupped Hunter's face, staring into his eyes as he took her body to a dangerously violent peak. She never broke eye contact, wanting him to remember what he did to her, what he could have had. It hit like a storm, sensations pelting her in long lush waves and spilling like hot wine through her blood.

Hunter couldn't just see Eden's climax, he experienced it, every shudder as she moved in his arms. The pulse and throb nearly undid him and he kept stroking her, kept kissing her, demanding the last slips of desire to come into his touch.

She was choking for breath when he felt her body relax and pulled her into the circle of his arms.

Her head bowed, it was a moment or two before she muttered, "Well, I don't know what to say."

He tipped her head back, giving her a crooked smile. "I guess I should apologize for taking advantage." Her bare breasts burned into his chest, an unnecessary reminder of what he'd done.

"Are you asking or offering?"

His smile widened. "Neither."

"You had a nightmare earlier," she said suddenly.

He frowned. That was unusual. He'd been trained to keep his dreams from fabricating and giving away secrets he shouldn't.

"I thought you would hit me you were so angry."

His expression fell. "Dammit. Did I hurt you?"

"You grabbed my arms and said 'You die tonight.'" She frowned. "What have you been doing all this time?"

Angered with himself, Hunter rolled away and stood, moving into the bathroom and shutting the door. He stared at his reflection, images flashing though his mind like ugly postcards. No, Eden didn't need to know the things he'd done for his country, for survival. Even he didn't want to remember them. He splashed water on his face, raking his fingers through his hair. How long could he expect her to accept no answers when she deserved more?

She knocked. "Hunter? Talk to me."

He yanked open the door.

At his dark look, Eden couldn't help but back away.

"Leave it alone," he said, then crossed the room. "I won't talk about it."

"My God, Hunter, are those bullet holes?"

"Yes."

She stepped toward him. "For pity's sake," she said, getting a good look at his bare torso in the light. "You're covered with scars." She reached to touch them and he clamped her wrist so fast she didn't see his hand move.

"Don't."

She twisted out of his grasp and he strode to the dresser, searching the drawers for a T-shirt. Eden stared at his back, counting at least six deep scars she could see in the lamplight. Who'd abused him like that? And why?

"You won't tell me…anything?"

Eden stood frozen to the ground as he yanked on the T-shirt.

"You must have been good for the CIA, close-mouthed, tight-lipped. All those national secrets to keep."

He turned to look at her. "I suppose you'll tell me what you mean by that?"

She shrugged. "You didn't share your feelings with me before, I shouldn't expect it now."

He gestured between them. "*We* have nothing to do with my life since I left Indigo."

"Must be nice to walk away from one life, start another, and never look back."

Pain slashed across his face. "I didn't want you to know what I was doing. I didn't want to think about you, Eden. Don't you get that?"

"Yes, it was rather clear when you never contacted me again."

"I don't want to get into this with you, not now. My family wanted something from me I couldn't give."

"At least you had a family."

Hunter closed his eyes for a second. "I'm sorry, it sounds trivial to you, I know." He moved toward her.

Eden backed away. "Are you ever going to be honest with me? I'm trusting you with my life, so I think you should give a little here."

"I can't tell you anything. So please stop asking."

What he'd done was secret and had to remain that way. Why he'd left her wasn't, but Hunter wasn't ready to wade into the mire of his mind right now.

Not when he was still feeling on edge for her.

"And I'm supposed to accept that and trust you?"

He faced her. She looked small and delicate in the moonlight, the silk robe wrapped tightly and her arms across her middle. It was her defensive posture, he realized.

"Yes, you are. Trust in one thing, Eden. I won't let you down. I will find Helene's killer."

"And then what? Will you go back to your duty without seeing your family?"

"Yes."

Her shoulders drooped. "That puts me in a rotten position."

"It's been seven years, Eden."

"You know they blame me for you leaving."

Hunter's features tightened. Keeping Eden out of

his mind for the past years had also kept him from recognizing the damage he'd left behind. "They don't blame you."

"You weren't there. How would you know?" She put up a hand and gave him a sour look, telling him she didn't want to hear his excuses. She went to the phone, ordering room service. The dawn was just breaking over the waterfront. It would be a beautiful day, Eden thought. Outside in the real world.

But in here, it had grown ugly with the reality of Hunter's life. And his lies.

TEN MILES AWAY on the edge of the city a young girl ran for her life, shouting at the empty streets. She screamed for help and no one came.

She ran and no one saw her. She clutched her belly, pain ripping though her. She didn't dare stop and ducked between two buildings. The walls swayed, her knees softening. She blinked, staggered, then ran out into the street. A cab screeched to a halt to avoid hitting her. Terrified, she took off, not remembering where she was, how she got away. Only that she had.

Her legs wobbled and, holding her stomach, she struggled to keep them moving forward. When she reached a lit street, she felt buoyed. It didn't last long. Someone grabbed her from behind and the crack on her skull came with a raging violence.

She dropped to the ground, feeling blood move across her scalp and pour into her ear, drip on the ground. He pulled at her arm, trying to lift her. She didn't have the strength to fight anymore. Car tires screeched, horns blasted. He let go, and all she heard was rapid footsteps fading into nothing.

I'm dying. Oh, God, I'm dying, she thought, then let the black painless void sweep over her.

THE SATELLITE PHONE rang at nine in the morning. Eden handed it to Hunter and moved away, sipping her coffee. He could barely hear Aidan Crew for the noise going on in the background.

"We found a young girl at dawn this morning."

"Alive?" His gaze flew to meet Eden's.

"Yes, thank God."

Hunter nodded and Eden sagged a little.

"She's badly beaten, drugged and has a concussion. The E.R. physician said she'd given birth less than twenty-four hours ago. A witness saw a man in dark clothing hit her, then try to pick her up. But as soon as he made himself known, the attacker fled. We haven't located him."

"I'm on my way."

"Not if you don't want to blow your cover."

"I don't plan on being seen." He hung up.

"They found someone?" Eden asked. "Is it linked to Helene's murder?"

"A girl who'd just had a baby, so I'd say— maybe."

"I'm going with you."

"No."

Her lips tightened and he knew she wanted to fight him on this. "I can get in and out easy enough, but you will attract attention. Especially if we're seen together."

She nodded, resigned to the fact that he was right.

Within a few minutes he was dressed and heading for the door. He paused, looking back at her. "Don't change the routine. If Harker calls or anyone asks, just say I'm in meetings."

"I think I can fake it," she said bitterly.

His features went taut. "We'll talk when I get back."

"I want the truth and I deserve better than what you're handing me, Hunter. So unless you want to be honest, there is no point in discussing a thing, is there?"

He didn't respond, letting his gaze slip over her for a moment before he left.

No, he thought, there was no point. There were some things he didn't want her to know.

THERE WAS A POLICE OFFICER outside the girl's hospital room, and though Crew didn't like it, Hunter needed to talk to the girl alone. He'd learned over the years that getting information from a source had more to do with delivery, the eyes and expressions than with what was actually said. He could get in through normal channels, but he didn't want this visit noted by anyone. He waited till the attending nurse left the room with a drug tray. He didn't have much time before the drugs would kick in.

Dressed as a surgeon in clothes he'd lifted from the storage closet, Hunter walked down the hall, snatching a stethoscope off a tray outside another room and after flashing his badge, he walked smoothly past the guard and into the private room.

The girl looked small in the bed, and as he neared, his chest tightened. She was a mess. Her head was bandaged, dark hair sticking out in sprigs and her jaw was swollen and scraped. Her hands lay at her sides, IVs in her arm and a nursing monitor on the tip of her finger.

She couldn't be more than fifteen.

She would survive, the physicians told Crew. It would take time, the trauma being the toughest to overcome, but she'd live. She was lucky. Hunter wondered if she knew how close she'd come to death.

He drew nearer, vaguely recognizing her. Quickly, he pulled out the photo he had of Senator Crane's daughter and compared it.

Alice.

Thank God.

He stood beside the hospital bed, reading the monitor, her chart. There'd been a high amount of narcotics in her bloodstream. It was a miracle she had even walked under her own power. He looked at the IV drip, the drug the nurse had administered dripping into the tube, figured he had about ten minutes before she was out cold.

She stirred, her eyes fluttering open. When they

fell on him, her heartbeat increased. The monitor pinged wildly.

"I'm not here to hurt you. I'm here to ask you a few questions, nothing more." He couldn't show her his ID. He wasn't supposed to exist.

For her peace of mind, he took a step back.

"You're Alice Crane?"

She nodded.

"Your father sent me to find you."

Tears came, and Hunter offered her a tissue, moving a little closer. "He's been very worried about you."

She looked at him, barely turning her head. "Are you Secret Service or something?"

He didn't say anything, letting her assume what she wanted.

In the pocket of the lab coat, he flipped on the recorder. He was already wired, and while the FBI would talk with her, Hunter wanted the information firsthand. Crew had pitched a fit over it, not trusting him, but Hunter didn't care. David Crane was his friend, and he had his priorities. It wasn't the first time he'd bent the law to suit him.

"Alice, do you know who did this to you?"

She shook her head, then winced.

"You're a long way from Washington, D.C. Why don't you tell me what you can? From the beginning."

She let out a long breath, and it was a few seconds before she spoke, her tone full of regret. "I'd had a fight with my dad over the baby, and when he threatened to lock me up, I took off. It was stupid, really stupid, and I had too much pride to go back with my tail tucked, you know?"

Hunter only nodded, listening.

"I was alone for weeks and couldn't get a job since I wasn't old enough. I lived on the streets till I met Duke."

"Duke? A boyfriend?"

"No, just a guy friend. Duke Pastori, he's not the baby's daddy." She looked away, touching her tummy, regret and pain swamping her features. "I was already a couple of months pregnant when I met him."

"Where did you meet him?"

"At a coffee shop near the clinic." Round eyes heavy with drugs peered at him.

"What happened then?"

"I was broke, and he took me to his place. It's on the south side of the city. Before the river."

She gave him the street address, but there were a half-dozen rivers and tributaries through Charleston, plus several streets with the same name.

"I stayed there, getting bigger every day." Her hand smoothed over her tummy, feeling for the baby that wasn't there, and the tears flowed. "When I was further along, I got sick, and he helped me. When I went into labor, he went to the clinic and brought back something for the pain." She looked at him directly. "That's the last thing I remember clearly."

Hunter nodded. Doctors didn't administer pain-killers to pregnant women unless it was under supervision.

"You don't seem surprised."

"You're not the first pregnant woman to be abducted, Alice."

"They took my baby." Her lip curled, her expression laced with so much pain, Hunter expected her to pass out any second.

He had to keep talking. "Do you recall anything about the birth of your child?"

As still as glass, she stared at the far wall. "No, not really. Walls, dark rooms. I heard voices, but I can't be sure. Everything I remember seems like a dream. Like I can't be sure if it was real or not." She sniffled, blotting her eyes. "I had a baby and don't even remember." She looked at him. "I don't even remember the pain. Duke wanted to put the baby up for adoption, but I didn't. I'm thinking he's done something with my baby."

She looked ready to collapse and Hunter redirected her thoughts. "Can you describe Mr. Pastori?"

"He's tall, not muscular or anything like you. He's got a whiskered soul patch, right here." She rubbed under her lower lip, then glanced around. "Where are my clothes?"

Hunter's brow tightened. Why was she so interested in her clothing?

"The police have your clothes, ma'am."

"I want them back."

"I'm afraid I can't do that. Was there something in them you needed?" Alice showed her first signs of rebellion by turning her face away. She was too weak to pressure and forensics would be taking her clothes apart for evidence by now. "Was Pastori the only person you saw while you were pregnant and living with him?"

She kept staring away, twisting her fingers in the bedcovers. "I'm tired," she complained in a whine. "Can we finish this later?"

Hunter's gaze narrowed. "No, we can't. Alice, look at me please."

She did, and Hunter narrowed his gaze, his expression harsh. It worked.

"No," she blurted tearily. "Harris came by a lot. Harris Bruiner. He's the one who really took care of me. I mean, I stayed with Duke, but Harris took me to lunch and bought me CDs, clothes and makeup, and made sure I ate right."

So she could deliver a healthy baby he could sell, he bet. "Was he a friend of Pastori's?"

"Oh, yeah, they were tight." Her words were slurring.

"Can't you describe Bruiner for me?"

She hesitated again. "He's old, like you. Dark hair, a little gray near his eyes."

Hunter hid a smile. He must seem ancient at thirty-three to a fifteen-year-old. "Did Bruiner hurt you, force you?"

Even behind the cuts and bruises, she looked appalled. "No, of course not, not him. He was wonderful to me."

Hunter recognized the adoration in her eyes. "Did he know who you were, a senator's daughter?"

"No, no one did. God, I'm not totally whacked, you know. I know that people would kidnap me 'cause of my dad."

"Someone *did* kidnap you, Miss Crane."

"Yeah, I guess." She rubbed her temple, her brow furrowed tight.

"What can you tell me about your escape?"

She looked up. "I got out of the room. I don't remember how. I ran. It felt like for hours. I think I slept in the woods, I don't know, but I remember getting inside the back of an old pickup truck."

"Did the driver know you were there?"

"I don't remember. I can't even remember the color of the truck. Just getting bounced inside the flatbed." Hunter's gaze flicked to her bandaged wrists. She fingered the gauze, her confused expression deepening.

"Do you know where you were held?"

"No."

"Was there anyone else with you?"

"I don't know. I told you, I heard voices, I don't remember what they were saying just…noise, muffled."

"When did you deliver your baby, Alice?"

"I don't know. I don't even know if it's alive. I can't tell you anything more. I don't have my baby and I ran! I ran! I was afraid and I ran." Her voice rose to hysterical pitch. "I don't remember anything! I don't remember!"

"Alice, calm down, shh," he said, taking her hand, stroking the back till she calmed. "It's okay, honey, it's okay. You did great. Now rest, rest."

She sighed into the pillows, her hands shaking miserably. "I want my father."

"He'll be here before tonight, I swear it." She lifted sad eyes to him. "I'm very glad you're safe, Alice."

"Thanks for looking for me."

"You saved yourself, you know? You were very brave."

She scoffed. "I was an idiot, mister." Her words slurred more heavily, the next ones dragging. "I just want to go—" she exhaled, closing her eyes "—home."

Hunter pushed a strand of hair out of her eyes as she drifted into a painless sleep. Quickly, he slipped out of the room as a nurse came down the hall. The police officer only nodded, keeping his post.

He kept walking, shutting off the recorder, and hoping Agent Crew had more to give him. They had to work fast.

Because Alice's baby was on the black market now.

With buyers already waiting—him and Eden.

Chapter Eight

"No wonder she wanted her clothes back."

Hunter stared at the photo he'd found in the lining of Alice's jacket. The fact that the jacket and her clothing were ripped and stained gave forensics a field day with material to process. But Hunter's concern was why, after all she'd been through, did Alice want to keep this hidden?

"This is useless," he said to Crew.

While a young man was visible in the Polaroid shot, the second figure was not. All they had was the back of his head. The man in the dark suit could be anyone. Which left them with zilch. This could be Bruiner or simply someone caught in the picture.

"Not entirely, we have a composite sketch artist ready to sit with Alice when she's well enough, and we can computer-enhance that." Crew nodded to the crumpled photo.

Hunter put the image of the battered, heartsick young girl from his mind, and accepted a photocopy of the picture and the shots of Alice's wounds. He slid them into a thin leather envelope containing his case files. As they spoke, SLED was at the address Alice had given him.

"Did I mention how much it pissed me off that you went to see her?" Crew stated.

"No, but go ahead."

"You could have been spotted, surely these people are watching you."

Hunter lifted his gaze to Crew's. "I've made a career out of blending in or disappearing, Crew."

Crew's features sharpened. "But the chance—"

"I had to take it. Getting it firsthand from Alice was more telling than a report."

"Yeah, I know the drill, so what did you learn?"

Hunter rested his rear on the edge of the desk. "She reveres this Bruiner." He flicked at the copies of the photos ready for the agents. "She didn't want to mention him and that she didn't want us to see that picture says she was trying to protect him. She trusted him, and when I implied he'd hurt her, she was in complete denial."

"That's not odd for someone who's been kidnapped or held hostage. Think of Patty Hearst."

Hunter made a sour face. "There's more to it than that. She has lacerations on her wrists, needle marks, aside from the injuries she suffered running through the swamps. They're the same injuries as Helene had, and we might have a stronger connection from Alice to Helene Carlyle's murder now."

Crew's brows shot up.

"Eden said that her sister had mentioned someone named Harry," Hunter said. Crew's features pulled taut. Clearly he'd forgotten about that.

"We're running a check on the name and starting a search of the countryside, matching dirt samples from her shoes."

That was the proverbial needle in the haystack. South of Charleston was more swamp and tributaries leading all the way to Indigo then onto Beaufort and Hilton Head. There were a million places to hide. "Alice's escape means they failed. She got away and they'll either attempt to kill her or they're changing operations as we speak."

Crew agreed. "One thing I've learned is that a criminal who's nearly caught is twice as cautious next time around." Crew glanced at the photos of Alice. "Have you called her father?"

Hunter shook his head. "I was hoping to have more to tell him first."

Crew gestured to the phone in the FBI office. "Take your time."

Alone, Hunter picked up the phone and dialed. He got the runaround for a second until he told the secretary who he was. Instantly David Crane was on the line.

"Hunter, tell me something great."

"She's alive, Dave."

There was a long pause and Hunter could hear him gasping for air. His voice trembled and Hunter's heart went out to the man.

"The baby?"

"She'd already delivered when we found her. The child is missing."

"Oh, God."

"Dave, she was hurt, bad. And we didn't find her, she found us." Hunter relayed the situation without revealing too many details of the case.

"What's your assessment, Hunter?"

"She escaped them somehow. Unfortunately whatever drug they gave her has left her with gaps in her memory. Probably a combination of rohypnol and ketamine. But it will take some lab work to narrow it down."

"Date rape drugs?"

"Or the like. It's not difficult to obliterate memory that will never be recovered. She has evidence of long-term drug usage in her system. We don't think it was self-inflicted." Hunter suspected she was kept nearly comatose until delivery. "And her attacker gave her one hell of a crack on the head, too."

"How is my little girl, Hunter? Really. You're the only person who'll give me an honest answer."

Hunter heard tears in the man's voice.

"She's scared and confused, in a lot of pain. Talking is an effort, her emotions are on the verge of overcoming her. She's telling us what she knows or what she believes is the truth."

"But you don't believe it."

"I'm not sure yet. Dave, she asked for you. I told her you would be here by nightfall."

"Thank you, Hunter, thank you."

"I didn't do much of anything, Dave, she freed herself. Seems she's got her daddy's backbone."

The senator's soft chuckle came through the phone, laced with tears of joy. Hunter said goodbye and hung up, his hand resting on the phone in the cradle for a second.

He never had the opportunity to make a call like that. Normally someone else in the agency did it. Often it wasn't good news. He was glad that today, hope shone.

HUNTER MADE IT BACK to the Mill's House hotel feeling a little buoyed by Alice's survival and the possibility of learning more from her when she was feeling better. He entered the hotel suite expecting Eden.

What he got was a dark, empty room.

Flipping on lights and laying his leather file case on the table, he found a note nearby. Running an errand was all it said. What errand? She was supposed to stay here and wait for him. Panicked that something might have happened to her, Hunter was reaching for the phone to call her cell when he heard the doorknob twist.

"Where have you been?" he demanded the instant she was inside.

"I left you a note, *darling,*" she said, unaffected by his anger as she stepped back to let the waiter wheel in a room-service cart.

Hunter waited till the tray was on the table and the man was gone before he spoke again. "You were supposed to stay here, Eden."

"Yes, I know, but I had my employee paychecks to see to."

He eyed her darkly. "Tell me you didn't drive to Indigo to sign them."

"No, I went to Overnight Express."

"What! Did you have something sent to you with your real name? Jeez, Eden. Do you realize these people—"

"Wait a minute," she cut in. "I sent an authorization to my accountant to sign the paychecks. Which I've done before, thank goodness, so the bank won't have a hissy fit over cashing them for my employees."

He just stared. "A hissy fit?"

"Yes, I mailed it to him under my company name, not my name, and it had to be done. I can't not pay my employees, Hunter, and if I didn't do it this way, I would have had to go back to Indigo to take care of it."

Hunter sighed hard. She'd been cautious, at least.

"Give me credit for having a brain."

"I do. I couldn't have done any of this without you."

"You would have found a way," she said. "So tell me what happened."

He gave her the quick version, and after a minute, she said thoughtfully, "If Alice Crane escaped some sort of holding cell, then you were right. They're keeping them hostage."

"All we know is that Alice was. She'd been heavily drugged and what memory she has isn't clear."

"She wasn't any help?"

"Enough to know there is a young man involved with this. Duke Pastori. Ring a bell?"

Shaking her head, Eden sank into a chair. "Helene and I didn't talk much in the last few months. How is Alice doing?" Her voice wavered and he knew she was thinking of her sister, wishing she'd survived.

"Lucky to be alive, really. They did a real number on her. God, she's just a kid. She should be on a cheerleading squad in high school." Just remembering the beaten and ragged girl made him furious and he rubbed his face, trying to banish the picture and focus.

Despite her irritation with him, Eden's sympathy won out and she gestured to the end of the table. "When Aidan called to say you were on your way, I ordered dinner for you."

Aidan. Not Agent Crew? The twinge of jealousy annoyed him, and Hunter went to the service, lifting lids. His favorite. Steak and shrimp. "Thank you," he said softly.

"I want to see Alice."

His gaze flashed up. "No way."

"But she's alone and scared and…"

"And I'm sure the baby ring knows she's in our hands. I'd bet they're scurrying to change locations right now, dammit." He sat and picked up a knife and fork, tired, yet too hungry to ignore the hot meal. He gave her a more detailed rundown on what he'd learned, including Harris Bruiner. When she badgered him with questions about Pastori, he said, "How about we wait till morning when Crew will have more?"

Eden didn't stop pacing. "All I can think about is that sweet-looking little old lady Margaret Harker and her people out there possibly searching for a young mother to snatch. For us."

"Yeah, me, too. And Alice's baby is up for grabs now."

"Could Harris Bruiner be Helene's Harry?"

"It's possible. Can you remember anything she said about him?" He chewed on rare steak, watching her pace at the end of the long table like a cat in a cage.

"She told me she was seeing Harry and when I asked about him, she only said he was older and that I'd like him. He was more my type, she'd said."

"Your type?" Now he was really curious. "What do you think she meant by that?"

"After you left, Helene was always trying to match me up with some man, and once she made a list of the requirements. Aside from money and a stable job I can't recall the entire list."

She shrugged, unable to stand still, and he could almost feel the turmoil rising in her. That he could sense it rather than see it struck him hard. There were still deep connections between them that years hadn't diminished.

"Try."

"She was young, so it included ridiculous stuff like a really nice car. But it was mostly attributes like makes me laugh, liked the same things, trustworthy, honorable, able to express himself…honesty."

Her sharp glance speared him, and Hunter realized she'd very nearly just described his exact opposite. He wasn't stable; he was in a different country every couple of weeks. And trust? At one time, she might have trusted him, but he'd destroyed that years ago. And he was certainly not being honest about his job.

"Was the list useful?"

"Are you asking about the men in my life?"

Putting the fork down, he sat back. "Yeah, I am."

"I haven't been a nun, does that satisfy you?" She put up a hand. "No, don't answer that." She brushed the edge of the table and sent his leather case file to the floor. He started to get up, but she waved him off. "I'll get it, enjoy your dinner."

She bent and when she didn't immediately stand, Hunter frowned and leaned out. "Oh, hell." He left his chair and went down on the floor beside her.

Crime scene photos were spread across the carpet. Eden held one, her gaze riveted to it.

"Eden, give it to me."

She didn't move, her hands shaking.

"Eden?"

Slowly, her gaze moved upward. Tears filled her eyes, her face carved with sadness and horror. His gaze snapped to the picture of Helene Carlyle's body, twisted and bloody, and he cursed, taking it and stuffing all the photos back in the case.

"You shouldn't have seen that, I'm sorry." He'd forgotten to zip it shut, dammit.

She sank to the floor, covering her face. "I wish I hadn't."

Hunter groaned, dropping the case and photos, and on his knees, he pulled her into his arms. They were vile pictures, a body violated in the worst manner.

"Oh, God, what he did to her," she choked, struggling not to cry. The police had only shown her a photo of her sister's face and told her some of the details. They'd left a lot out.

"I'm so sorry, baby."

"I want to kill someone," she said, her voice hardening. "I've never had that feeling before Helene was killed, but I want to see someone *die* for doing that to her."

"We'll get him, I swear it."

"I really wish you'd stop making promises you can't keep!" She twisted to look at him, then stood as he did.

Her words spoke volumes, their hit direct. "You're still ticked at me for leaving."

She whipped around, her eyes flashing. "No. You're *wrong*. You didn't want me and I accepted that a long time ago. Don't fool yourself that I've been pining away for you. I didn't have the time with a rebellious teenage sister to feed, clothe and house. But since that charity ball, I've only wanted one thing…an explanation as to why you didn't have the guts to face me."

His features went taut.

"I deserve at least that," she snapped. "I'd loved you with everything I had and you abandoned me as if I never mattered."

Hunter felt the arrow of her words pierce his heart. "It wasn't that simple. I did love you, Eden. God, it killed me to leave."

"You didn't *leave*," she delivered coolly. "You vanished off the face of the earth!" She went for the kill, tipping her chin up, her green eyes spearing with anger. "You were a coward."

"Now wait a minute—"

"You never loved me." She walked over his words. "That's what hurt the most. I loved you madly, Hunter. And perhaps some of it was the security and family that marrying you offered, but I loved *you*."

Even when I was sleeping, echoed in his mind.

"So much that if you'd asked," she went on, "I would have gone with you."

"Into this life? Eden, I don't even have a home."

"Like I said before, it's a moot point, isn't it?" She shook her head, the sad resolution in her eyes slaying him where he stood. "God, I wish you'd just stayed away."

Turning, she walked sedately to the bedroom and quietly shut the door. No storming off, no slamming.

Just dignified pain.

The lock snicked closed, sounding like a gunshot in the quiet room.

Hunter pushed his fingers through his hair and gripped the back of his neck. In moments he was pacing, tearing off his jacket, then snapping off his tie. Silence permeated the lavish suite with an emptiness that seemed to stab him.

I wish you'd just stayed away.

Coward.

She was right, he had been cowardly that day, but it stung more to hear it from her. He'd spent the last seven years trying to erase the shame of it, taking risks that had earned him the scars on his body, being the one man his superiors could count on to get the job done, no excuses.

Because the only woman he'd ever truly loved hadn't been able to count on him. More angry with himself than her, he went to the door and popped the lock, pushing it open.

She was curled on the dainty striped sofa, staring out the window. Tears slipped down her cheeks. The instant she saw him, she shot off the sofa.

"I don't want to be near you right now." She headed out.

He stepped into her path. "Too bad." When she made to go around, he caught her by the arms, holding her there. "You wanted answers, now you'll have to hear them. I made a tough choice. It was cruel and selfish, I admit that. I was twenty-six. I knew my choices would hurt a lot of people. Especially you. But staying was killing me!"

"How come I didn't see this?" She pushed out of his touch, hurt in her eyes. "Why did you hide it from me?"

"Because I wasn't unhappy with loving you, Eden. I was unhappy with myself."

She searched his features. "Make me understand, Hunter."

"I didn't like the man I was. I needed to prove to myself that I was more than the son of Sebastian and Olivia Couviyon. That there was more to me than a three-hundred-year-old lineage."

"Why didn't you at least talk to me?" Her eyes turned glossy, the sight lashing at his heart.

"It was hard enough to leave. I knew if I saw you just once more, I'd have stayed."

Her pain was palatable, stinging him. "Was that so bad?"

Something inside him broke apart and he gently pushed a loose strand of her hair off her cheek. He was grateful she didn't flinch away. "Yes. I'd have ended up making you miserable, too."

Eden let out a breath, relaxing her folded arms. Moving to sit on the sofa, she peeled open her memory. Had she ignored the signs? Hunter and his brothers had been raised differently, their needs came second to the town their ancestors had founded, and though the four Couviyon brothers were formidable, it was Hunter and Logan who were pushed to the foreground. Each had been forced to take on heavy responsibilities at a young age, whether they wanted them or not.

While Eden had thought it was somehow an honor back then, Hunter must have felt as though a keyless cage was closing in on him. Or else he would not have left so suddenly.

"Eden, say something," he whispered, settling down beside her.

She shrugged, staring at her lap and looking incredibly frail. "In a way I'm relieved. I thought that I wasn't good enough for you and you didn't love me enough to tell me so."

A tear dripped onto her fist and remorse slithered through him, drifted across his features.

"I'm sorry, Eden." He passed his hand over her hair, tipping her chin and staring deep into her eyes.

Eden felt the draw of them, the pull that had always yanked at her heart.

"The truth was, I wasn't good enough for *you.*"

Her gaze ripped over his face.

"Under that shyness, you were so much stronger and braver than me. When your parents died, you climbed back up, charging ahead. You never looked for anyone to fix things for you. You just did them."

"I didn't have a choice."

"Yet you wouldn't take help from me, so who were you really depending on?" When she blinked, his lips curved just for a second. "I wasn't the man you needed then, Eden. The way I left proved it. I felt trapped because staying came with tight strings and measuring up to a three-hundred-year-old standard. I had to find my own yardstick first."

Staring at her lap, Eden realized Hunter's self-worth had been so linked with his ancestors, his family name, that without them, he hadn't known who he truly was, what he could accomplish. And he'd left to find out. "So how are you measuring up now?"

"That depends on you."

She swiped at her cheeks, and looked at him, confused. "Me?"

"Can you ever forgive me?" he asked quietly.

Her gaze roamed over his handsome face, the young man she'd known before obliterated with experience and age. While she'd buried the past years ago, she realized today that it had clung to Hunter after all this time. Shamed him. It didn't make her happy; even in her worst moments she'd never wished anything bad on him. He held a special place in her heart and probably always would.

There were some men a girl just didn't get over completely.

"Yes."

He smiled. Wide and all the way to his eyes. After the remoteness she'd seen in him since the charity ball, it was like a little gift.

"Thank you," he whispered, his voice trembling, his fingers intertwining with hers.

When he leaned closer, his gaze on her mouth, Eden gravitated toward him. His tongue slid with luxurious patience across her lower lip, a sweet taste away, and she waited, anticipation spiraling through her blood.

This is so different, she thought, *even from last night.*

He closed the space, his mouth pressing deeply over hers, surging on the edge of wild a second before the ringing phone broke the spell. Easing back, he muttered something she was probably better off not hearing and went to answer it.

Within moments, their entire world changed directions.

Again.

Chapter Nine

"We found a blood pool," Agent Crew said on the other end of the line.

Hunter's gaze snapped to Eden's and she rose off the sofa. "Where?"

"Northwest, about seventy miles from the city limit. It's a lot. Some hikers found it. Stepped in it actually. We hadn't had rain, but the animals had feasted on it, tore up the ground around it."

Despite all he'd heard and seen, Hunter's stomach turned over. "Your opinion?"

"It's the killing ground," Crew said. "There are two areas where we found depressions in the ground and blood. They covered their tracks well. We have a partial footprint and found cigarette butts a half mile down the road, they're fresh.

That's DNA, Hunter thought.

"How'd you find this site?"

"That's the thing, it was near the fire road."

"A kill zone in full view of anyone passing by?"

"Yes."

"Man, that's cocky."

"Or desperate. We have searchers moving through the woods now, but it's too dark, we'll try again in the morning. Jeez, I'd love a decent footprint, anything. This widens the area."

It did more than that. It proved the women had been transported. A dead body left a trail of DNA. "We need clothes, a vehicle, something to link us to the killer. Because we have nothing without a perp," Hunter said.

"We have an APB out for Pastori, he'll turn up. The place Alice said she lived with Pastori is occupied by a newly married couple. They bought the place empty and for cash."

Hunter hung up and looked at Eden. She had such a hopeful expression he hated to crush it. He relayed the information as gently as he could. She simply nodded, listening, keeping her composure. He went to his leather case in the living room, slipping out one picture. She followed, and he handed it to her.

"That, we believe, is Duke Pastori."

Eden stared at the photocopy. The young man looked like any other. About twenty-five, tall, slender, dark hair. He wore trendy clothes, had a pierced ear, and a little bit of hair under his lip, which to Eden looked like a smudge of dirt. "Why didn't you show me this before?"

He arched a brow. "You were already upset with me."

She gave him a quick smile of admittance.

"Who's the other person?" She peered closer as if that would make the picture focus.

"We don't know. Might be Harris Bruiner."

A little shred of hope surged through her before reality hit. "We'd be reaching, the picture is too obscure." Hunter agreed as she handed the picture back. "And why would someone who was involved in a black-market baby ring even allow his photograph to be taken?"

"I don't think they knew. It's a Polaroid, so there's no negative. And its light out, no need for a flash. Plus neither is looking at the camera. I'm betting no one knew Alice had the picture. She hid it in the lining of her jacket."

Eden was thoughtful for a second. "Helene said that Harry was older and I'd like him." She gestured to the picture. "That man looks distinguished and older, Helene's idea of being stable." Eden smiled to herself. "She didn't see much beyond first impressions."

"Alice admitted mostly the same and she didn't want us to find that. When she realized eventually we would, she capitulated. I'm betting that's him, but I doubt the name's real. Which doesn't get us anywhere beyond over thirty-five and dark hair."

Hunter moved to the side bar, pouring himself a drink, holding up a glass in offering. She nodded and he selected her favorite almond liqueur. She took it, flipped on the CD player, then kicked off her shoes before curling up on the living-room sofa. Soft jazz filled the suite.

"What's your theory on this?" she asked him. "I know you have one."

He eyed her over the rim of the glass. For a second she reminded him of a fairy queen sitting on a mushroom. "You aren't going to like it."

"And that's made a difference how?"

He sat down on the couch, but kept himself at the far end. Eden shifted, leaned her back against the armrest and pillows, then stretched out her beautiful legs. Hunter wanted nothing more than to run his hands all the way up them. So he focused on her question.

"I think Pastori was a hook for the girls. The pregnant women were young and alone, feeling ostracized. Then along comes some sympathetic, good-looking kid, with rock-star quality. He's flashing money, the girls are desperate from what we'd learned, and they fell for it easily."

Hunter took a gulp of his drink, knowing what he had to add wasn't going to be pretty. "I think, with the exception of Alice, Pastori was the lure and it was Harris who gained their confidence, affection, then maybe he got them pregnant."

"You mean he set out to impregnate them? Like picking them off a shelf? Good teeth, pretty eyes? She'll make great babies?"

He nodded and watched her fury build. She threw her legs off the sofa.

"What kind of man would be so cold as to do that, then sell his own child?"

"A dangerous one."

She was breathing hard, her body going as tense as an iron bar. Her face bore the horror of a thousand untamed thoughts. "Helene knew this man! She trusted him! He killed her, you think he killed her, too!"

"Eden, take a breath."

Eden stared blankly, her mind somewhere else, thinking of Helene, that she hadn't been alone, desperate. She'd had a sister, dammit. "Why didn't she come to me? Why?"

Hunter scooted closer, rubbing her back. "Slow breaths," he told her, and she obeyed. He pushed the crystal tumbler to her lips. "Take a drink, baby."

She did, and the warm spill of liquid down her throat softened her nerves.

He took the glass, setting it on the coffee table, and kept rubbing her back. "You okay?"

She nodded and looked at him. "How can you do this? How can you learn such awful things and not want to go running off like a vigilante?"

"I imagine, just like Agent Crew, I step back from it. See it like a movie. Victim, villains, associates, suspects."

"Is that how you do whatever it is you do for the CIA?"

He debated answering for a second, relaxing into the sofa, his arm on the back. When she curled toward him, he met her gaze, a warning in his blue eyes that what he was about to tell her could never leave this room. "I remove items from the black market. Don't ask, I won't give you specifics," he cut in when she opened her mouth to ask. "I try to find as many players that are involved, then select one who has the most access, is trusted enough to get me where I need to be, which is near the source. I worm my way into their lives by any means available. Sometimes it's blackmail, threats, masquerade." One shoulder lifted. "Or convincing someone low in the ranks that they are serving a greater good of the free world."

"Hunter," she said stunned. She suspected from the nightmare last night that his methods of convincing involved less talk than action.

Hunter kept his gaze on Eden, waiting for her judgment.

"It sounds like a con game."

"It is. Well, it was," he said, looking confused for a second. "Till I realized Helene was a victim." And that Eden would be in danger. He'd been the only one risking anything before and had had little to lose.

"And now?"

His gaze locked with hers. "I knew Helene. I taught her how to drive, remember? I keep that in the back of my mind now. The victim has a face this time."

"Can you tell me how you found the trail here?" He eyed her.

"I won't tell a soul, I swear." She crossed her heart, zipped her lips.

"It was by accident, really. I was in Istanbul, to

buy a specific item off the black market. A man I was cultivating offered me a virgin as a gift in the sale."

Her eyes widened.

"I accepted. I figured in my hotel room was better than raped by some terrorist."

"What did you do?"

"I sold her."

"What?"

"To another U.S. agent. It was an auction, for women. Young, very scared and drugged girls. The arms dealer who'd offered her was highly amused. It engaged his trust. The other agent won the bid, which was a setup, of course, and he got her out of the country. She should be home with her family by now."

Eden smiled with relief.

"By doing that I'd established myself as a player, my contact was the supplier. It brought me closer to the other girls and where they kept them. When I found the girls, that's when I learned about the infants. In some cases, they'd used the girls to bring the babies over the borders, sold the girls, sold the babies. They were threatening their families. Some were American, British, Spanish, a few Middle Eastern. The American girls were from all over, but the pickups for the babies were from around here."

"It sounds very dangerous."

"Weigh the risks against the price the victims pay and it isn't."

She was infinitely proud of him just then. "I guess

not. Did you get the other *items* off the black market, too?"

He simply nodded. He would never reveal that he'd blown the place to hell after he had.

With a sigh, she leaned her head against his shoulder. "It's very courageous, what you're doing."

"I've done some things that aren't."

"I suspect you had to, Hunter," she said softly.

He tipped back to look her in the eye.

"I won't judge you, if that's what you're waiting for."

"Eden, I've done—"

She covered his mouth. "I don't need to know. I know the kind of man you are, and that's enough."

"You still say that after what I did to you?"

"Oh, Hunter," she groaned. "We all make mistakes and regret them. But we can't change them, just learn from it all."

His lips curved. "When did you get so wise?"

"Last Wednesday. Humor me till I get it right."

He chuckled, his arms slipping off the sofa back and wrapping around her. For a second, he just savored the feel of her beside him. Then he shifted and she eased back to look him in the eye. He stared, as if memorizing her face.

"What?" she said.

"I was an idiot to leave you."

A bell of triumph rang through Eden. "You left a different woman." She leaned into him, loving that his arms went around her. "And I loved a different man."

Hunter didn't ask if she could love him now. He knew he wasn't staying. She knew it, too, and yet, feeling her against him gave new meaning to the words *home fires burning*. Buried deep was the need for her, something he'd gone without. He'd had sex with several women, some for the job, some not. But he'd never come close to anything he'd had with Eden. She was the only woman he'd ever made love to, and having her in his arms was oil on the flame that had been flickering since he'd seen her at the ball. She'd been driving him crazy since.

His gaze dropped to her mouth, then flashed to her eyes.

A sharp sting of anticipation skated through Eden. "Are you going to kiss me or just stare?" she murmured.

Hunter's smile was slow and roguish. "You want me to?"

"You'd be surprised at what I want, Hunter Couviyon."

She planted a quick, hot kiss on his mouth, then stood, slipping away.

"Oh, that's cruel."

She smiled back at him and Hunter's arms felt so devoid of her warmth they almost ached. Confused, his gaze followed her as she went into the bedroom. After a second he followed and found the bathroom door closed and heard the sound of running water.

Hunter backed off. She was just teasing him, he

thought, then corrected himself. Eden never teased, it wasn't in her. Right?

Hunter busied himself with covering the room service tray and moving it near the door, then sat at his computer, updating his records with the interview with Alice. Something about Alice's behavior nagged at Hunter, but with Eden dominating his thoughts, it was difficult to focus. He could hear the splash of water, his mind taking off with tantalizing images. He typed almost viciously to obliterate the memory of last night, of feeling her climax in his arms. Of what it would feel like to be trapped inside her again.

Oh, man.

He slammed his eyes shut, but that only brought the memories back tenfold. Rubbing his face, he focused on the screen. He had been at it for nearly fifteen minutes when a sound interrupted the silence.

He frowned, scanning the room. It was a funny little chime, the tango, he realized, and searched for the source.

It was the cell phone in Eden's handbag. Opening it, he answered the call.

"Who's this?" a man demanded on the other end of the line. The voice sounded familiar.

Hunter looked at the number display, memorizing it. "Eden's occupied."

"How about you let her decide that?"

Covering the phone's mouthpiece, Hunter moved to the bathroom door and knocked. "You have a phone call." Then he pushed open the door.

Eden was neck deep in bubbles and frowning. "I thought I shut it off."

"Check next time." Hunter waited till she dried her hands and took the phone.

"Hello? Temple! Hi."

Hunter's brows drew tight. Temple wasn't a common name and since it was an Indigo exchange, Hunter assumed she was talking to his youngest brother. He didn't know what to think about that, but jealousy was the first emotion he recognized.

"Just an old friend, Temple. He answered the phone for me." Eden shooed at Hunter, but he simply braced his shoulder on the doorjamb, shoved his hands in his pockets, and listened.

Eden scooped bubbles to cover her breasts, conscious of Hunter's study. She could almost feel his fingers slipping over her. Temple was asking about the man with her. "I don't think that's any of your business," she said, lifting her gaze to Hunter.

His expression was carved in stone, showing her nothing. But she could detect a little flexing in his jaw, as if he was grinding his teeth.

Temple talked, but Eden wasn't really listening. She couldn't take her eyes off Hunter. In a snow-white shirt and tailored black trousers, he looked incredible sexy. She recognized the way his gaze bored into her, the tension in him that stirred heat through her blood.

He wanted her. Right now.

The question was, would she let it happen?

"Hum? Ah—I needed the time to be away, alone," she said absently. "Tell everyone I'll be home as soon as I can."

Hunter's expression darkened.

"I have to go, Temple. I'm fine, really." She said goodbye, then shut off the phone.

"Temple? You're seeing my little brother?"

"He's not so little anymore, Hunter." She laid the phone on the stack of thick towels and knew that wasn't the answer he wanted.

"What if he comes after you?"

Hunter's comment reminded her that he thought of work before anything else. "He has far too many women on a string for that."

Hunter arched a brow.

"Your brother is a playboy."

"Are you dating *him?*"

She blinked. "Do you honestly think I'd go from one brother to another?"

She wouldn't, Hunter knew Eden was too classy for that, but he had to know. "What is he to you, then?"

She lay back in the tub, bending one leg and draping it over the edge. It was all Hunter could do not to sink to his knees and start licking a path up to her thigh. His body had gone on full alert the instant he'd seen her in the tub; now he was a man on the edge.

His patience hanging by a thread, he asked, "Answer me, Eden, before I drag you out of that tub and shake it out of you."

"We're friends," she answered. "Just as I am with Logan and Nash, Nash's wife, Lisa, Hope Randell. And most of the people in Indigo."

Hunter let out a relieved breath. The thought of Temple anywhere near Eden made him want to drive to Indigo just to punch his lights out. But he didn't have the right to be mad, to want, to be jealous. He'd given her up.

But part of him still claimed her. She'd given him her virtue, promised herself to him, and though he'd ruined that, Eden was still somehow—his.

This was nuts, he thought. Get a grip. Eden isn't the one-night-stand kind of woman, and if he understood anything, it was that.

His gaze jerked to her when she picked up the handheld sprayer from the rack and turned on the water to rinse.

Eden glanced at him, and he noticed that the bubbles were disintegrating by the second. "The water's cold, I'd like to get out."

"Who's stopping you?" His gaze slid over her, liquid-hot and branding.

She met his gaze and Hunter saw something flicker there. A challenge. A message. He read it. Then, bold as you please, Eden stood, turning the sprayer on herself. Hunter lost his breath, lost any control he might have thought he had as she rinsed bubbles from her body, revealing every naked inch of the woman he'd once loved. And lost.

"Don't ever dare me, Hunter…"

His gaze climbed up her glistening body to meet her cat-green eyes.

"…you'll never win."

"Who wants to win?" he said, taking three steps and scooping her from the tub.

His mouth was on hers before her feet left the bath, her wet body crushed in his arms. The kiss was volatile, consuming them in seconds and sending shock waves of desire that propelled them toward the inevitable.

"Is this something we'll regret?" she said against his mouth even as she hurriedly thumbed open the buttons of his shirt.

"Probably." He backed her against the marble sink, the cold stone beneath her bare bottom making her gasp. He drank it, ravishing her mouth, her warm skin sliding under his palms till he filled his hands with her breasts. His fingertips slicked over her nipples.

She moaned and he loved it, loved the way she tipped her head back, offering herself to him. He gaze moved over her face, her throat, down to his hands covering her smooth flesh. One thought shot through the erotic haze.

He wanted her in his bed. Consequences be damned. She had his emotions locked in her fist.

All Hunter saw was the woman he could have loved for a lifetime and lost because he needed to discover himself.

He stepped back. "I don't want to hurt you again."

Eden saw his torment and spoke fom the heart. "I won't kid you. I have feelings for you, Hunter. Some old—" her lips curved "—some new." She stepped out of the steamy bathroom, slipping on a terry-cloth robe. "But I'm not trying to recapture the past."

He made a frustrated sound. "Believe me, neither am I."

She unpinned her hair. His shirt was opened. As she drew closer, she slid her hands under the expensive fabric and pushed it off his shoulders. His breath snapped in, his hands clenched at his sides.

"You're killing me, you know that?" His shirt whispered to the floor.

She smiled softly, her palms splayed over his muscled chest. "Do you remember that night on the river, Hunter?"

His features went taut. She'd come to him a virgin, a little scared, but so sure of her love for him, he'd been humbled. "I'll never forget it."

Laying her body to his, she sank her fingers into his hair, urging him down. "Well." Her tongue slid over his lips and his breath shivered softly. "I can almost guarantee this will be much better."

Chapter Ten

Hunter groaned as he covered her mouth with his, his strong arms trapping her against him. It was a slow, deep kiss, persistent and spilling with hunger.

And with emotions he'd left behind, locked in a cave out of fear, the absolute terror that he'd never feel them again and he'd made the biggest mistake of his life by walking away from her. So he didn't acknowledge them, didn't let himself relive them.

But they'd seeped through the cracks like hot gold slithering down a mountain, burning him with the loneliness he'd never let close. And the reason for it was in his arms, wanting him, kissing him, and Hunter struggled for patience to reacquaint himself with Eden and with some lost part of his soul.

She'd been the only one. The only one. Her hands slid around to his back, glazing over the scars that were ugly harsh reminders. Yet her fingers soothed, tips digging as if to banish them into the night.

He wanted more of it, more of her, and he tugged at the robe sash, opening it, then sliding his arms inside. Her skin was warm and scented with spice, and she moved into him, shrugging off the robe.

"I never let myself think of this, or you, ever," he said, his kiss driving her back over his arms.

Her hips ground as he dipped his head to lave at her nipples, his tongue slicking in deep circles before her drew the rosy tip into the heat of his mouth.

Her breath skipped; his one hand cupping her breast as if he could take more of her into his mouth. Then he moved lower, nipping at her ribs, the swell of her hip, her belly, and lower, coming close to her heat but never touching, making her twist and squirm. He tortured her slowly, telling her how beautiful she was, how if he'd let himself remember this he'd have gone mad. He traced a path upward, demanding a taste of every inch of her, his hands busy shaping her contours. He reveled in her softness, in the pure femininity displayed for him. He rose to stand behind her, his hands closing over her breasts and she laid her head back on his shoulder.

He whispered, "Open your eyes," and she did, shocked to see them standing before the tall cheval mirror.

Eden's gaze met his in the mirror, the heat there dark and devastating her already charged senses. She wanted his touch, wanted him pushing inside her, and she tamped down her impatience and watched his broad tanned hands move over her paler skin.

"You're so beautiful," he whispered very softly in her ear, then kissed her throat. "Look at you."

One hand slid lower, down her flat belly to dive between her legs. She inhaled and flexed in his arms, and Hunter parted her, watching her face, seeing the heat rise in her as he delved into her softness. She was wet and hot, the knowledge driving his desire for her to incredible heights.

He felt humbled again, just to touch her, to know she was willingly in his arms again. She reached up to push her fingers into his hair, the erotic pose snapping at his control like the jaws of a beast. He saw the real beauty of Eden in that moment, so intense, an innocent trust lying far beneath the exquisite display of naked curves.

His heart clenched and he felt unworthy. Then her body shifted, urging him, giving him everything—again.

He didn't deserve her. He didn't deny himself.

It was new yet familiar. Nothing was the same, and Hunter knew before he first kissed her that it never would be again.

"I love touching you," he whispered and Eden looked, watching him cup her breast, stroke her center.

Then she turned in his arms, her bare body fused to his, her lush mouth and tongue sparring with his and pulling him to the edge. She shaped the hardness pressing against the fabric of his trousers and he ground her palms to him, wanting more, always more. She opened his belt, the soft slide of the zipper erotic in the room filled with moans and soft breaths.

She dipped her hand inside, enfolding him, and Hunter felt his restraint slip another notch.

"Eden," he managed, lifting her off her feet and advancing toward the bed. Her smile was full of feline grace and power as he lowered her to the down bedding. She knew he was weak for her. He planned to reverse the tables.

With his mouth, he traced the valleys and hollows. With his hands, he mapped her curves, his tongue dipping into her navel he'd been dying to taste again. She arched on the bed, her fingers in his hair and he shifted between her thighs, scooping her bottom and bringing her to his mouth.

With his thumbs he spread her, devouring her completely, his tongue making quick dips and dives into her delicate flesh. She cried out, begging for him to come to her. He refused and her body fell into a pool of sensation that coated her skin, simmered through her blood. His tongue flicked and drove, and when she was near her climax, he receded, then did it again, taking her up the lavish peak and letting her dangle.

She gripped fistfuls of sheets and bucked against him, her breathing labored—as if trying to catch up with the rushing pleasure he created. She came to the brink again and he hesitated. "Hunter, you're making me crazy."

"That's the whole point," he said, easing back to strip out of his clothes. She rose up, grabbing at him.

He paused. "Wait, we need—"

"No, we don't," she said, pulling him into her arms, between her thighs. His arousal pressed to her center, teasing, slickening. Poised.

His gaze locked with hers. Something new and bright rocketed between them. As if nothing had come before now. Then he pushed, filling her in one smooth thrust. He went perfectly still, not trusting himself to shift, his body quaking with the need to pound into her. To claim her when he didn't have the right.

He swallowed, smoothing her hair back. His voice wavered as he said, "I've missed you, baby."

She touched his lips, his jaw, her eyes burning. "Show me." She moved, stealing his thoughts, the wet retreating glide of him sending pulses of sensation out to her fingers and toes. He sank into her, deeper, and with each push, she rose to greet him, to capture more of him. More of the man who'd first stolen her heart and had never really given it back.

Flesh met and the craving grew.

Skin glistened, their moans whispering through the elegant room.

Gentleness slid swiftly to untamed desire, hot and piercing.

Hunter thrust, and she bowed beneath him, clamping him, hurling him toward ecstasy. He slipped his hand under her hips, lifting her to him, grinding, energy neither could control unleashing between them in a fury of hunger.

Eden couldn't catch her breath.

Hunter couldn't get enough.

His hips pistoned. Her feminine muscles clawed, trapping him with white-hot passion. She cried out his name, begging him for that final push, and he met her gaze and gave it, thrusting once, twice, holding her suspended on the edge of rapture. Bodies flexed. Breaths scattered.

Her eyes sparkled and flared as a tumble of sensations ruptured in her, a throbbing explosion that shoved him over the edge. Hunter quaked as pleasure roared up his spine like a wild beast set free, spilling hotly through his bloodstream and into her.

"Eden," he moaned and swept her up off the bed, taking her with him as he fell back on his haunches, grinding her down on him. Her arms and legs clamped around him and he held her as the quiver and twists of her seized around him. He buried his face in the curve of her neck and held tight, unable to move, never wanting to.

She'd been his deepest pain and his darkest desire. Only in sleep had he let himself think of her, let himself regret and want. The path he'd chosen was worthy, but none of it mattered now. Not when Eden was in his arms.

Slowly the rush faded to pulses, those to soft throbs and he lifted his head, smoothing her hair back. In the dim light, he kissed her, her face in his palms.

He would have sworn there was a sheen to her eyes.

And he knew.

This time when he left, it would kill him.

MARGARET HARKER called the next morning, asking Hunter and Eden to meet her again. Though they'd expected it, hoped for it, the interesting change was that the address was different from the last. This time it was in a newly restored area of Charleston.

"Is your wire turned on?" Eden said. "Can Agent Crew hear us?"

Hunter shook his head as he angled the sports car around a curve toward Margaret Harker's new address.

"Good."

He arched a brow in her direction.

"Well, it's bad enough you can't wipe that smile off your face, I didn't want the FBI being privy to anything more."

"I'm allowed to smile."

She scoffed. "You haven't yet."

"That was my game face."

"Oh, really?" She laughed, leaning toward him, and he caught a whiff of her perfume. "Well, before every breath is on record, I just wanted to tell you that last night—"

"—*was* better than before?"

Her smile wore the seductiveness of the night before and Hunter instantly felt the power.

"Yeah." Incredible, she thought. So different.

"It was more than that," he said, clasping her hand.

But that's where it will stay, Eden thought. She wouldn't allow herself to read more into last night. She'd had it set in her mind from the start that he was leaving. She didn't want to focus on more than the pleasure they gave each other and the case that brought them together. She let go of his hand so he could shift, thinking she could really torture the man when both hands were occupied.

"Stop looking at me like that, Eden."

She blinked, then grinned as he shifted uncomfortably in the seat. With a Cheshire-cat smile, she stared out the window.

Hunter took a side street, very aware of the woman beside him and the FBI van behind them. His car had a tracking beacon, they couldn't lose them. He would much rather be back in bed with Eden, but even he was wise enough to know that they were here to do a job. No matter what.

He glanced her way. He'd woken with her in his arms, naked and warm, and for a while he'd simply watched her sleep. It was sappy, but the first time he'd ever made love to her had been outside by the river, when he'd taken her to Charleston for a weekend. He'd been the teacher then, and not very good, and she'd been so innocent. But even that didn't compare to last night.

Eden was a woman who knew her own power and he'd had the pleasure of it at daybreak this morning.

He glanced at her profile, and frowned. "What's the matter?

She looked at him, giving him a small smile. "You think Harris Bruiner or whatever his name is killed my sister, don't you?"

"We don't know that. It could have been another. We don't know if that man exists or if he's someone else completely. The man in that picture could be anyone."

"But still Harry or Harris? We already know he was nurturing to both women. And a knife killing, is that what you call personal attack?"

He nodded. "Usually it's an axe to grind against that person, they want to see them die."

Her expression fell.

"I'm sorry, baby, but murder is never pretty."

"No, I asked. What about the others?"

"The other three were killed with a knife, fairly large, serrated edge. They were found naked and badly decomposed. One was submerged in the river so little evidence could be retrieved. As far as we know, no one was searching for them."

She made a face. "Someone has to know them, Hunter. You don't pass through life without *someone* remembering you."

"True, but without prints to match, or a missing persons report, there is little to go on. Decomposition tells us when they were killed, not who they are. The FBI have a forensic pathologist reconstructing their faces for the public. I wish we could broadcast them, but in the middle of a sting to buy a baby, the perps would close up shop and head out."

"I disagree. I'm not saying risk exposure, but Margaret Harker has two houses, why not more? She has a method to her madness and might not do this constantly, she might fade into the background for a while, or just take her victims from some other nearby area."

He frowned. "Go on."

"She'd string the would-be parents along for as long as possible to make them more and more desperate so she'll get the most money. A million for a baby, two? Anyway, she milks the customer long enough to check them out thoroughly, or has someone else do it. Like Roxanne Mitchell, the lawyer. No harm in making inquires. At least that part looks legit, right?"

He nodded.

"Harker has a comfort zone and it's right here. It's the reason I haven't left Indigo. It's home, and though I had the chance to go elsewhere, I—"

"When?" he interrupted.

"I had a friend who offered me a partnership in his restaurants."

"Why didn't you take it?"

"Mostly because he wanted a little more than partnership."

Hunter's gaze narrowed, a ping of jealousy hopping through him.

"Indigo has everything I love, the people, the small-town quality, the waterfront. I'm comfortable. Unless there is a good reason, I have no real desire to take off to parts unknown permanently. A vacation is enough. And I've been to ten different countries." She said the last in flawless French.

"So what are you getting at?"

"I'm sure they could keep up this black-market ring from anywhere. But they aren't, they haven't been. It's been long enough that you tracked babies from Europe to here. Margaret Harker is from here, has lived her for most of her life, Hunter. I checked."

"Eden, the slightest thing could alert them."

"I didn't do anything more than look a couple things up on the Net. She was in the list of town patriarchs. So she's trusted. No, she'd stay right here and just change tactics. It's familiar ground."

She waited for him to agree, but he didn't.

"You said yourself that Helene was not killed where they found her. What if she was killed right here in Charleston? Alice ran, but she didn't know anything before that. Maybe she was here all the time? Since she'd already had her baby, they might have been transporting her somewhere farther from the city to be killed and that's when she escaped. Maybe that truck she mentioned is what they'd used. We know for sure she was tied up and drugged."

"Alice's memory is very disjointed," he said, adding weight to her theory.

"Where were the other three girls' bodies found?"

"All different areas. One was thirty miles south. Two were farther northeast."

"But Alice surfaced here, just a mile away. I think they are basing here. With Harker."

Hunter shook his head. "Criminals do not always follow the pattern of normal folk, Eden, but I have to agree with you."

"I'll bet you twenty dollars that Margaret Harker has been doing more right under the nose of the mayor."

"You're on." He pulled to the side of the road, a couple of blocks from their destination. She looked confused till Hunter handed her a small plastic packet.

She frowned, taking it, turning it over. "Is this what I think it is?"

"A room bug, yes. I want you to plant it in the office."

"Why me?"

"Because if we're discovered, you can be doing something like straightening your stockings or looking for an earring. I'll look more conspicuous if I'm bent under a table. It has a backing that'll stick, just don't put it near the computer."

Eden opened the packet, shaking out the tiny chip, then wedged it between her breasts.

Hunter arched a brow, eyeing her breasts and remembering how they felt in his hands, against his mouth.

"Easy access," she said, pinkening as he pulled into traffic.

Chuckling, he drove the next block and pulled

into the driveway. Together, they walked to the door. Hunter held her hand, her nervousness evident by her tight grip.

Margaret Harker answered the door with a bright smile, then escorted them into the parlor of the house. Despite the new address, the style of decor was virtually the same.

They hadn't spent but a moment in the parlor when Margaret ushered them into a small, darkly lit office. It had one window, facing the street and driveway, yet it offered little sunlight in contrast to the shelves burgeoning with books. It was a law office, he thought, glancing at the titles.

"I want to show you some pictures."

"Pictures?" Eden said, curiously looking on as Margaret pulled out a thin photo album.

"Of course."

"Oh, I hadn't realized there would be photographs."

Harker gave her a patient, grandmotherly smile and laid the book out, pulling a chair close and telling Eden to come look.

Eden didn't hesitate and sat, her gaze scanning each picture as Harker flipped through the pages to the one she wanted.

"These other photos are of children already placed?" Eden asked.

"All my angels get a good home, I make sure of it."

Eden glanced at Hunter, who moved to stand behind her, his size imposing.

Harker's glance was annoyed, but he stared her down, daring her to tell him to move. She complied and when Eden's sharp inhale broke the short silence, he looked down. "Oh, Hunter, look at her."

He bent, studying the picture and knew why she was so drawn. She met his gaze over Harker's head, and Hunter read it.

This is Helene's baby.

"This baby," Eden said, stopping Harker from turning the page. "I want this baby."

"Oh, dear, I'm so sorry. That one is not available. I forgot to take the photo out before you arrived." Red-faced, Harker flipped back the protective plastic, snatched the photo and slipped it into the desk drawer.

Eden's shoulders drooped, and Hunter felt the strength of her disappointment.

"You're certain?" she said woefully.

"Yes. I'm so sorry," Harker said, patting her hand. "But look at the others."

Eden continued to look at the other pictures, appearing disinterested for a second. "No, I want that baby," she said clearly, pointing to the desk drawer.

Hunter met Harker's gaze, challenging her.

"I can't. I'm sorry."

"Eden," Hunter said and she looked up at him, her eyes tortured with the knowledge that the child in the photo was gone. "Let's go, darling. You're too upset."

Eden rose.

"Wait, wait," Harker said quickly. She chewed

her lip for a second, eyeing them both then said, "I'll be a moment." She locked the album in the desk drawer, then walked out the door to the parlor.

Hunter came to her, pulling her close.

"Hunter?"

"Play along. I don't see any cameras." He turned a bit, kissing her face, one eye scanning the room. "But let's not chance it." Hunter stepped back, smiling down at her, then moved away. He was tempted to run his hands over and under lamps and desks, pull at the books on the shelves.

Eden behaved as if she were adjusting her clothing, and fished out the room bug. She glanced around, as if studying the decor, till Hunter inclined his head to the desk. She let her shoe slip off, then bracing her hand on the desk to adjust the strap, she pressed the bug under the lip of the desk, guest side. Margaret's footsteps sounded on the hardwood floor and Eden popped upright, looking scared. Hunter rushed to her, taking her in his arms and kissing her.

Kissing me silly, she thought as his strong arms closed around her. She sank into him, barely hearing Harker open the door and clear her throat.

They parted, Eden blushing and Hunter red-faced. Harker looked amused.

"What you want will be yours."

A smile exploded across Eden's face and she grabbed at Hunter's hand. "The mother signs over the rights, correct?" she asked.

Harker nodded.

"I—we want proof," Eden said.

Margaret met her gaze, her soft granny eyes gone narrow.

Eden didn't care. "You have to admit, Miss Margaret, it would be cruel for the birth mother to demand rights for the child years from now. A baby we've loved and raised as our own would be torn from us and I won't allow that cruelty to be put upon my child."

"If that's what you want."

"We do. Also, I want medical history, birth certificates and parent history, too. No names if that suits, but we need to be on the alert for something down the road."

Harker didn't confirm or deny her, and then Eden said, "We want this before we hand over the money."

"Eden," Hunter said, thinking she might blow the whole operation right now.

She looked at him, laying her hand on his chest and inching closer to him. "Darling, you didn't get to be a very wealthy man by not seeing the obstacles ahead."

Hunter brushed the backs of his knuckles along her jaw, nodding, then looked at Harker, waiting for an answer.

"I'll have to check on this with…" She didn't finish her sentence and left the room again.

Hunter didn't say a word to Eden, glaring down at her.

"You're mad, aren't you, darling?" She sighed.

"I could never be mad at you, dear." He said that through gritted teeth.

Harker returned, and Hunter waited, his heartbeat staggering when she said nothing till she was seated.

"Your terms will be met."

Eden squealed with delight, throwing herself in Hunter's arms and over her shoulder, he met Harker's gaze, silently warning her to not let his wife down.

The woman didn't bat a lash as she rose and ushered them to the door. "I'll be calling you soon."

"The redhead," Hunter said, looking down at Eden and fingering a lock of her hair. "I want a daughter I can love and pamper, like my wife."

Eden's gaze locked with his, and her eyes were so questioning, he hurried her out of the house. He didn't want to think of his feelings, they felt raw and tender right now.

But as they drove back to the Mill's House, he said, "You were great in there, Eden."

"Funny, you looked a little upset at my demands."

"I was, but if we'd gone blithely by, she would have been suspicious. A woman who was really looking to buy a baby would have been prepared and would have asked those questions and demanded written proof." He glanced at her, taking a right turn. "Do you really think the baby is—"

"She was a ringer for Helene when she was little," Eden said excitedly, her heart clutching at the memory.

"You sure you're not seeing with wishful eyes?"

"No, I have a picture sitting on the mantel in my living room of Helene at two months old. She hated that I kept it there. It was my father's favorite picture of her. I've seen it every day, Hunter. Trust me, that little girl was my sister's baby."

Chapter Eleven

Eden moved around the *Southern Belle's* baby shop in Mount Pleasant, cooing appropriately over frilly bassinets and clothes so tiny it was hard to believe they'd fit anything but a child's baby doll. Underneath the facade, he could sense she was holding on to her anger by a thread.

The ring worked both ways, though he'd done his best to stop it in Europe, there was no telling how wide it stretched in the U.S. Helene's child most likely was out of the country.

He didn't want to remind Eden further. So he sat in the corner of the shop in a chair he thought would shatter under his weight and watched her.

He couldn't help it. Her bright-green sundress was made of something slinky, hugging the curves he'd got to know last night, but it was the woman inside it who kept his attention. He was proud of her. She'd been a step ahead of the game with Harker, and though he'd hate to disappoint her if they didn't find her sister's baby, he never wanted to see her hurting again.

He never wanted to be the cause.

He'd turn over every last clue, every last stone to put that baby in her arms.

His gaze followed her as she pulled out toys and baby essentials; Hunter was boggled by all the things a kid needed. The customers, most of them pregnant, kept giving him strange sympathetic looks as they strolled past.

Apparently men shouldn't be concerned with anything more than getting women pregnant and paying for the baby for the rest of their lives. Hunter's features tightened when he realized he'd left Eden so suddenly years ago that he hadn't considered he could have left her pregnant. No birth control was foolproof.

Watching her now, a small part of himself imagined Eden pregnant—with his baby. Something new and frightening torpedoed through him right then.

He realized it wasn't such as scary idea.

But would she trust him enough to let him into her life? Did he want to go home to Indigo? A handful of thoughts tumbled through his mind, the least of which was that if he wanted more than right now, he'd have to leave the CIA or keep her in the dark. It was not a great life. He was in the field for months at a time, and he'd already told her he didn't have a house, an apartment, nothing. He wasn't supposed to exist. That included not having anything in his possession that could be traced back to his past. Sting operations were his forte, his job. Masquerading to get what he needed, pitting all the players against each other the way he wanted it.

But Eden didn't play his way. She'd refused to stand aside; she'd jumped right in, doing every thing necessary to make this work. She'd fooled him already with her independence, her strength and intelligence. And worse, her forgiveness. It would be easier to leave if she hated him still. Then he'd know where he stood. Now he didn't.

He could sift through feelings and facts, but when it came down to it, only Eden's heart mattered. Neither of them was in a position to make any life-changing decisions.

Not with the killer and a missing baby between them.

Over a rack she met his gaze, then frowned, moving toward him. "Are you all right?"

"Can we get out of here?"

She smiled, sympathetic. "Yes, we can."

She gathered up her purchases and inclined her head. He all but leaped to her side, and left the shop. Inside the car, she slid closer, and he bent to kiss her, the passion of the night before quick to ignite. Hunter forced himself to move back.

"Eden, I think you have to try not to get your hopes up over this child."

Eden knew he didn't want to see her disappointed. "No matter what happens, Hunter, I'm thrilled that if that's Helene's baby, it's alive and with people who'd pay a fortune to have her." Her eyebrows knitted. "I had horrible dreams that the child had died, and I was truly alone."

Eden relaxed into the seat and put the window down. The October air slipped over her skin and Hunter gently tipped her face toward his, his mouth lying warmly over hers. The simmer between them rose to a boil in the space of a minute, desire bubbling on the trip from Mount Pleasant to the hotel.

Her hand rode up his thigh, and Eden was considering climbing onto his lap when the car stopped in front of the hotel. Abruptly the FBI driver opened the door. She blushed, smoothing her lipstick from his mouth and loving his sappy look. While the driver was frowning, the doorman was grinning widely.

Hunter hopped out, then pulled her from the car and into his arms. Kissing her lightly, he instructed the doorman to have the packages delivered to their room.

"In an hour," Eden tossed over her shoulder as they walked into the hotel. Her gaze slid to Hunter's.

Hunter recognized the smoldering look on her face. He'd bet his own matched it, and he couldn't wait to get her alone. And naked. Inside the elevator, he immediately pressed her to the wall, his mouth crashing over hers, his hand mapping roughly up her spine. She responded instantly, sliding her hands up his chest and into his hair.

"Your behind in that dress is making me an idiot."

She grinned. "I'll have to remember that."

"I want you."

"Do tell." She smiled against his mouth as his hand found its way under her sundress, cupping her bottom, and pulling her against his groin. "Oh, yeah, that's a clear message," she panted.

"You sure? Because I could be much clearer." To prove it, he hooked the leg band of her panties, tracing it from her bottom across her hip then lower, and when his fingers slid near her center, Eden thought she'd burn into ashes right there.

He dipped a single finger into her center and she quivered in his arms.

"Oh, my," she said against his lips, ravishing his mouth and he pushed deeper, stroking the bead of her sex in slow erotic circles. Her nipples firmed and she let out a little pleading whimper just as the elevator pinged.

Hunter stepped back, his face expressionless as he grabbed her hand and tugged her rapidly down the hall to the room. As he slid the key card through the sensor, she was behind him, reaching around, molding him.

He choked, sliding the key card back and forth in the lock.

"Two can play at this," she whispered.

"Man, I hope so." The key wouldn't scan; Hunter considered it a personal affront and didn't think he'd make it inside.

But once they were behind the closed door, passion exploded.

Eden loved the wild way he kissed her, the trail

of clothes they left behind. Hunter cursed when his shirt buttons wouldn't open, then just ripped the expensive fabric. Eden tortured him, strutting toward the bedroom wearing nothing but green high heels.

He didn't let her get that far, grabbing her back and depositing her on the table.

"You drive me absolutely insane," he said.

"A good place to be." She spread her thighs.

"Then you're coming with me," he said, and entered her, deeply, thoroughly, grasping her hips to retreat and plunge again. And again.

She trapped him with her strong legs, his body pulsing almost savagely into her, and she grinned, teasing him. He bent to latch on to her pert nipple. He drew hard, and Eden came unglued, her body swarming with sensations, the deep thrust of him inside her making her muscles contract. Suddenly, he scooped her off the table and backed her against the nearest wall, pushing into her, retreating enough to make her squirm, then gliding home.

In seconds they fell to the floor, his momentum pushing them across the soft carpet, mouths meeting and challenging, devouring with unmatched greed.

"Eden," Hunter moaned, breathless, meeting her gaze, watching himself disappear into her. She smiled up at him, touching his face, pulling him down for a passionate kiss.

It crept up on him, took him by surprise, the tight draw of rapture snapping with electricity, stealing his composure. He shoved and she accepted, begged for more, he pulled her onto his lap, grinding her down onto him, pushing and pushing, touching where they joined and feeling her rippling throb like a live wire wrapped around him. The crash was hard and devastating, the calm like a drop off the edge of the earth.

Eden's skin was still humming, her breathing hard, she looked at Hunter and they both burst out laughing.

Then he kissed her, slowly and deliberately, the heated passion stirring inside her again. Once they were sated, time was on their hands—till the next call, the next meeting.

Hunter cupped her face in his palms, kissing her with tender patience, and when he leaned back enough to look her in the eyes, something worked in his throat, closing it up. He got a serious smile in return. She understood what she meant to him, he to her. Neither would voice it. To put words to feelings was dangerous; they had a right only to this instant.

Hunter didn't want to shatter the protected moment.

Eden wanted to wrap herself in it and hide from the world.

He pressed his forehead to hers, smiling, then inclined his head to the debris of clothing. "Think I'll be charged by the FBI for ruining a silk shirt?"

She snickered, and he stood with her in his arms, carrying her into the bedroom, then lying with her on the bed. For long silent moments, they lay tangled in each other's arms.

Till the phone rang.

Hunter cursed under his breath, reaching for it. Phone in hand, he froze, inhaling sharply as Eden slipped from him and off the bed. His gaze followed her as she stepped into the bathroom. He planned on joining her.

Agent Crew's timing stunk and Hunter barked a hello into the phone.

"We listened to the tape. Nothing Harker said to you will hold up in court," Agent Crew said.

"I figured that."

"The only thing damaging is what you two said. Eden was amazing with Harker. She really thinks she saw her sister's baby?"

Crew had heard the conversation through the wires in the car. "Yes, but I don't believe it."

"It's not impossible."

"We have to think it is." He looked over at the bathroom door, and could hear the shower. "It'll kill her if it's not."

"I'm sending you a composite from Alice's description. She was uncooperative, even her father had little influence. We had to show her some…evidence of the other women."

Hunter's brows rose. "And here I thought *I* played hardball."

"We needed that picture and Bruiner ID'd. Now we have it, we're running it through the computers.

The tail on Roxanne Mitchell and the investigation of her finances proved to be a dead end. She represents the richest of the city, and any association could be dissolved by a good trial lawyer. She didn't do anything illegal, except make a couple of calls and we can't prove what was said. The Ramsgates, on the other hand, have recently adopted a child. But the paperwork is clean."

"A state agency?"

"No, private adoption. But it's solid."

"Dig deeper."

"Couviyon—"

"Dig, Agent Crew. We're missing something."

Crew told him to hold on, and Hunter heard excited voices in the background.

"Guess who just turned up in Alabama on felony rape charges?"

Hunter simply waited for the bomb to drop.

"Duke Pastori."

"That means he's fled the ring."

"I'm going down there myself to find out why."

"Lucky you."

Hunter hung up, his mind turning over leads, yet when Eden called to him, he pushed them aside for later. He'd have all night to sift over gruesome details. Right now, he had other priorities.

WHILE CREW FLEW to Alabama, Hunter had to meet with the FBI and SLED teams. In secret. He'd left Eden to keep up the pretense of shopping for a coming baby. He didn't want to let her out of his sight, but he had no choice. She drew attention. Together, they drew more.

In an unmarked dark-blue car, nothing like the luxurious sedan with a chauffeur, Hunter headed north to a meeting with the rest of the team. Traffic snagged him in a short gridlock, and he took a side street, making turn after turn to avoid the buildup near the bridge. He frowned; the area looked familiar. Realizing he was close to Harker's last address, he slowed down, doubling back and watching from the corner a half a block away.

He waited till he was nearly late for the meeting, then started the engine. As he did, the door to the small Charleston-style house opened, and a man in a dark suit stepped out on the porch. He glanced around, even looked right at Hunter's car. Hunter didn't bother hiding; the glass was tinted too dark for the man to see in.

He sized him up in one glance. Dark hair, thirty-five, the unyielding posture of boarding schools or the military. The quick efficient stride said he didn't waste time. His clothes were expensive, well-tailored.

The man walked to a car and quickly climbed behind the wheel. Hunter memorized the license plate, and called it in. A cruiser would follow him from another direction. Hunter didn't want to chance losing him and pulled onto the road, tailing him for a block, then veering right. He contacted the SLED officer, and their positions, tracking the sedan. Hunter would bet his career that was Harris Bruiner. The house had been empty since he and Eden had met with Margaret Harker. Harker had returned to the first home and hadn't left.

At a distance, Hunter trailed the maroon Cadillac. He took a side street as the man turned onto a main avenue off Meeting Street, close to the hotel. Hunter parked, watching as he got out, bought a newspaper from a vending machine, and was nearly to the car when he turned back to the small coffee shop.

Hunter called in the position to the FBI and waited. He took out his binoculars, wishing he had a long-range camera, and focused in on the little shop. The man sat in the corner, his back to the wall, but near the front. Easy exit, no one coming from behind, Hunter thought. Defensive posture. For ten minutes he sipped coffee from a foam cup as he read the paper, and Hunter made radio contact with the officers and agents, positioning one on the street in plain clothes. The policemen smoked a cigarette, behaving as if he was waiting for a ride. The radio crackled, and the officer tipped his head toward the shirt mike.

Don't, Hunter thought. *He'll know you're wired.*

When the banter between the cops scattered through the airways, Hunter spoke into the transmitter. "Cut the chatter, he's got a disposable cup. When he pitches it or leaves it, one of you get it. If it's been discarded in a public receptacle, it's ours. Be careful, it's evidence. We need that man's DNA."

The suspect folded the paper with a strange methodical precision, smoothing the edges, then, God love him, wrapped the paper around the cup and discarded both.

Bingo.

Hunter could have taken him out easily at this range with his side arm, but he needed to confirm his identity. The man looked like the composite lying on the seat beside him, but then, Hunter had been mistaken for his older brother Logan a zillion times when they were growing up.

Hunter waited till the man was in his car before he pulled into traffic. In the rearview mirror, he saw the officer move to the trash and take the coffee cup. Hunter said a silent prayer, something he hadn't dared do for years. He needed a DNA match, the skin samples under Helene Carlyle's fingernails were from her killer. Her struggle to stay alive was going to help nail the bastard.

To the wall.

SOUTHERN BELLE's was one of the finest baby shops in the Charleston area. It catered to the pampered infant and toddler.

Eden was tired of shopping for a baby she didn't have when her arms were aching for her sister's child.

Her heart felt just plain bruised.

Though Hunter and Agent Crew insisted they were closing in, she wasn't so sure. But Hunter felt the situation warranted she carry a weapon. She'd refused. She didn't know enough about weapons to want to be near one. He'd spent the better part of an hour this morning convincing her that for her own protection, at least a tazer was necessary; the palm-size zapper she could handle, he was certain.

Her arms loaded with packages, she left the shop and hailed a cab, wanting a hot bath and to get out of the high heels. She was in no mood to hear another detail about the murders, Pastori or blood pools.

She just wanted the baby safely away from these horrible people, and to go home. The closer they got to finding the killer, the sooner Hunter would be leaving.

Muscles squeezed down on her heart, and she stared at her clenched hands on her lap as the cab rolled away from the curb. Silently, she admitted she wanted him to stay, to give them a chance, but she wouldn't dare ask him. She wouldn't even let herself dream about it. He had an important career and Indigo was no longer the kind of place Hunter needed to be happy. She knew because he'd confided in her, trusted her with more than he probably should have. Though he painted a colorful picture of beautiful cities across the globe, she could read between the lines. He dealt with the world's deadliest people, made himself a part of their lives.

It scared her to think of him going back to that, because he seemed to enjoy it far more than was sensible.

Needing a distraction, she looked out the window, then frowned at the scenery. A quick hard chill skated up her spine. *Where are we?*

"Driver, this isn't the way to the hotel." She slipped her hand into her purse, fingers closing around the tazer.

"It's a short cut, ma'am," the cabby drawled. "The traffic is stopped on the bridge and backin' up into town."

She held on to the tazer as they rode through narrow neighborhood streets, pausing for school children. Eden smiled as a little blond girl skipped her way across the street. Then her gaze went beyond.

"Driver, go slow please."

Eden's attention was riveted to the two-story house she and Hunter had been in a week before for their first meeting with Harker. And hurrying down the flower-lined sidewalk with an ample-size cloth-covered basket tucked under her arm was Margaret Harker. Eden glanced around for FBI surveillance, but didn't see anyone out of the ordinary. She looked back at Harker.

The aging woman hauled herself into a small sports utility vehicle, which looked odd since Harker wasn't a big woman. When she pulled out of the drive, Eden instructed the driver to follow the car, and almost laughed at how that sounded.

He glanced back at her, his expression saying "you've got to be kidding."

"There's a twenty in for you if you keep out of

sight." She winked and, grinning, he obeyed. He drove south of Broad Street, turning onto Tradd Avenue. The SUV slid to the side of the street in front of a huge two-story Georgian home graced with four columns and surrounded by beautifully manicured gardens. It had to be least two hundred years old and, considering the location, she knew it was worth over three million. The old woman got out, and like an efficient little bird, hurried up the cobbled walk to the front steps. She knocked and, without preamble, was immediately let inside.

Eden didn't see who had answered the door, and told the driver to keep going as she noted what she could; the address, that there were no other cars and the house had only off-street parking. When they were headed back toward Meeting Street, she pulled out her cell and called Hunter.

"Where are you?" he demanded.

She told him what she'd seen.

"Dammit, Eden, get back to the hotel and stay put. The FBI are watching her."

There was a strange edge to his voice. "What's wrong?"

"Nothing."

"Who are you trying to fool? Because it can't be me." He didn't answer. "Hunter," she said, "I saw her and had to follow. I thought I was—"

"You were putting yourself in danger, and I've been doing my best to see that that doesn't happen. Get back to the hotel."

Annoyed at his demand, she cut off the phone without saying goodbye and sat back in the seat. "The Mill's House Hotel, please."

Margaret Harker had looked like a woman on a mission, and Eden didn't want to guess what that mission was.

Chapter Twelve

"The Ramsgates are not home, ma'am. Only me and the little miss."

Margaret's smile hid her annoyance. The Ramsgates knew she was coming. She always checked on the care of the children she'd placed. "When do you expect them?"

"Any time ma'am. Would you care to wait?"

Margaret nodded, and took a seat in the parlor.

"Would you like to see the baby?" the nanny asked.

"I'll wait for permission from the parents, thank you. Are they out a lot?"

"Yes, ma'am. But I love taking care of little Sylvia."

Margaret smothered her frown. She knew well and good that the Ramsgates were socializing a great deal. Her daughter had seen them several times at the Oaks Country Club and twice in town dining out. Without their baby.

It was the reason she was here.

"Help yourself to the fresh service of coffee there." The nanny gestured to the sideboard. "The Ramsgates always have some when they return, night or day, even when it's a hundred outside. Creatures of habit, I guess."

When the nanny left, Margaret moved to the secretary desk tucked in the corner of the parlor. Mrs. Ramsgate's date book was open. She thumbed through it, mentally noting that nearly every day was filled with some social event. Only three had anything to do with a child. Not even a christening.

This was unsatisfactory. Margaret didn't give a child to a couple who didn't truly want it. The child had to be the focus or they'd suffer. She knew, she'd seen it before. It was the reason she placed unwanted babies with those who could give them a comfortable life and lots of love and attention.

Their slut mothers would have given them nothing but harshness and ridicule. It was cruel to leave the children to that kind of life when she could do something about it. And she had, for nearly forty years.

She'd been schooled by her own mother, and she'd groomed her daughter and now her granddaughter to the task. There would always be promiscuous girls who'd get themselves pregnant without a husband and produce babies for her clients.

Her loyalty was to the babies first.

But she regretted this placement and the longer she waited, listening for the soft cry of a child, the more agitated she grew. She was sitting in the parlor sipping coffee from heirloom china when the unsatisfactory parents finally arrived.

The couple, wearing matching golf outfits, stopped short when they saw her.

"Oh, Miss Harker," Paulette Ramsgate said and looked nervously at her husband, Chase. "We thought we recognized your car."

Margaret greeted them warmly, liking them regardless. Pity. "I just wanted to see how you were doing with your new addition."

"Oh, she's a good baby, hardly a bother at all." Paulette Ramsgate swept into the parlor, carelessly tossing her handbag on the floor. "We just adore her."

"May I see her?"

"Of course, I'll ring for her nanny."

They couldn't even take her to the child? Did they ever think of the child first? The darling thing was so young, she was likely sleeping. Did she even feed her baby herself?

"No, please don't. I'd rather not disturb the baby if she's resting," she said pointedly. "May I go up and peek in on her?"

"Of course," Chase Ramsgate said, moving to the coffee service.

Margaret flipped back the cloth covering the basket. "I've brought you some of my fresh-baked muffins to enjoy with your coffee." Chase Ramsgate had a sweet tooth, she recalled, and he practically lurched at the breads.

"I'll take one to the nanny, too." She wrapped a muffin in a napkin, and didn't waste time climbing the stairs. She followed the sweet smell of baby powder to the richly appointed nursery where she found the nanny sitting in the rocker, reading a magazine. She offered the muffin and the woman seemed grateful for the break.

Margaret leaned over the crib and her heart lurched. A downy fluff of red hair peeked out from under a soft blanket trimmed in velvet. Carefully, she lifted the child in her arms, cooing softly as the infant fussed and wiggled into a comfortable position.

Margaret patted her gently, dropping a kiss to the top of her head, then walked briskly down the hall, not giving the nanny writhing on the floor in convulsions a second look. She met the same display downstairs, the Ramsgates choking on their last breath.

"She's hardly three weeks old and you leave her? If you're already tired of her in your lives, then you don't deserve her."

Neither reached for her, neither cried out. The poison had done its job.

Margaret removed the cloths from the muffins, revealing the softly padded bedding ready for the tiny baby. She tucked the child into the basket, then slipped the linen over the opening. She gathered up any remnants of her visit, placing her coffee cup near Paulette, who'd yet to pour herself one, carefully wiping off the prints and lipstick stains. She picked up the basket, stared blandly down at the couple twitching on the floor for a moment, then marched out the front door.

THE INSTANT Eden was inside the hotel suite, Hunter was in her face.

"Are you crazy? You could have been spotted!"

"I wasn't. She didn't think she was being followed and I was in a cab."

Hunter raked his fingers through his hair, cursing a blue streak.

Eden winced. "Really, Hunter, don't you think you're overreacting?"

"No, I'm not. Not when I saw Bruiner, or who I think is Bruiner." Her eyes widened. "What would have happened if the old woman had recognized you?"

"I would have fast-talked."

"Eden." He struggled for patience. "These people have killed. Not just mothers. We found the body of the clinic worker this morning."

She blinked. "The young man from the free clinic, the one who'd passed the information on the victims?"

He nodded. "He was out on bail. He shouldn't have been released for just this reason," Hunter gnashed. "It looks like suicide. According to the officers in the holding cells, the kid was despondent and on the verge of a breakdown." Guilt was a mighty weapon, Hunter thought, pacing a few steps.

Eden's face was marked with such misery, Hunter gathered her close.

She laid her cheek on his shoulder. "How many will die before we find them? We have to catch them. They'll kill anyone in their way."

"Why do you think I was so worried about you?" The gravity of his fear smacked him in the chest and Hunter tightened his arms around her. She tipped her head back, nipping at his mouth.

"You think this will soften my anger?" Even as he said it, he nibbled back.

"I was hoping. I am prepared to do more."

It was all he needed. He kissed her, deeply, madly, his hands fisting in her clothes as if to push her into himself. As if to brand her as his and keep her safe.

He eased back enough to press his forehead to hers. "Don't do that again," he said fiercely. It was the first time in nearly a decade that Hunter had been scared out of his mind. "If you're not with me, I want to know where you are, twenty-four seven."

"I promise. It was actually pretty exciting." His expression went black. "I have a license plate, an address," she said quickly. "And there weren't any other cars, there isn't a garage." She handed him a slip of paper. "Harker was let inside without question."

"She may have called ahead." Glancing at the address, Hunter made a couple of calls. "No, don't go in yet," he told the agent on the other end of the line. "We don't have probable cause and going in like cowboys could blow this operation sky-high. Put a man on the house and watch. And let me know the instant Crew returns or calls."

He hung up and went to his computer, telling her about seeing Bruiner as he typed in the house address she had written down. It wasn't under any real-estate listings, so he went the next route, matching the car license number with the address.

"Chase Ramsgate."

"Oh, my God." She rushed to look over his shoulder.

He tapped into SLED files. "No police reports, not even a speeding ticket."

"Maybe Harker was just visiting."

He eyed her skeptically.

"She *is* a social creature, Hunter. What about Bruiner, where did he go after the coffee shop?"

"They're still tailing him."

"Did he look like the composite?"

"Enough. But Alice will be the only one who can identify him visually."

"Did her father take her home?"

"She's not well enough for travel yet."

"What did Bruiner look like?"

He twisted to pull her onto his lap, quiet for a moment. "He looked like me." Instantly, she met his gaze. "The expensive suit made him look distinguished, and the gray around the temples added to it. He carried himself very erect, stiff. At first glance you'd think he was a banker or a wealthy businessman." Hunter wondered why the man hadn't been seen in social circles, then considered he didn't want to be noticed. This wasn't about money and prestige. This was about the act of killing and why.

"Almost fatherly?"

His brows furrowed. "What are you getting at?"

"I've been trying to understand what Helene would have seen in him. She usually went for the bad-boy types, you know. I'm thinking she saw a future, dependability, and she'd needed that after our parents died. She and my dad were very close." He made a face. "I know it sounds weird, but every girl who loves her father looks for someone with those qualities because that's really the only steady male influence they've had. My dad was a strong man, faithful, willing to sacrifice his own wants for his wife and family. He treated my mother like a queen and loved her very deeply." She shrugged. "Perhaps Helene was looking for that and thought she'd found it, unfortunately, in Bruiner."

Hunter was already shaking his head. "This man is nothing like you'd think. He's a fraud down to his polished shoes."

"We know that, but she didn't. First impressions were everything to her, remember?"

"The profilers said he most likely harbors a hatred for women."

"Okay, then why? What happened to make him hate unwed mothers and want to sell babies, any babies?"

"You've been thinking about that a lot?" he asked.

She nodded, pushing off his lap and going to the coffee service. She fixed two cups as she spoke. "Maybe he was abused. Or maybe he was a bastard. His mother unwed."

"The profilers believe that. Their theory is that he was likely abandoned or suffered awhile with a mother, but no father. They believe he's saving the babies, but can't differentiate between the ones he's made and the ones he didn't." He accepted the china cup, wishing for a mug as she sat in the chair beside him. "It's a cycle to him. He'll keep repeating and Harker doesn't care. He's giving her what she needs, and he's cleaning up the mess by killing the mothers and disposing the bodies for her, too."

"I hate to think that the father of my sister's baby was a serial killer, Hunter." She stirred the cream in, then let out a long, tired breath.

"Maybe he's not." Hunter had his doubts.

"I'm hoping, really hoping."

He reached over, clasping her hand. "That's all we can do right now."

His own words sounded hollow. He'd never lived on hope. He lived on facts and the next move, the next push in the direction he'd needed. But hope? That was something he left for his bosses, for the families of the victims. But now hope was a part of this investigation, and he was in deep.

He had as much at stake as anyone.

And looking at Eden, he didn't want to lose.

His satellite phone rang and Hunter heard the three words he didn't want to hear.

"We lost him."

Holding on to his temper, Hunter grilled the agent on the other end of the line. Bruiner had left the maroon Cadillac at a Citadel mall. Agents had followed him inside and the man had vanished into the crowd. They'd posted a man on the car and at each exit, but after the mall had closed and only the security personnel were left, the car remained where it was parked. Although agents had dusted it for prints, there wasn't a single one on the car, yet they insisted he wasn't wearing gloves and hadn't taken the time to wipe the car down. Hunter knew a handful of ways to keep prints from showing, and a niggling suspicion rose.

"Get the security camera tapes, all of them. Look for a face, not clothing, because in a mall he could have stolen a change of clothes and slipped past." *I would have,* Hunter thought. They were back to square one, and the really bad news? It was possible that Bruiner was on to them.

HUNTER PULLED UP to the fast-food restaurant and ordered a soda, then drove to the rear of the lot. When the SLED agent got into the car, Hunter demanded the report, the reason he'd dragged Hunter out in the middle of the night. The loss of Bruiner had put him in a foul mood to begin with. The night didn't improve.

"They're dead. The Ramsgates. The coroner says about seven or eight yesterday evening. They were poisoned, along with the nanny. Even if an ambulance had arrived moments later, they would have been too late."

"The baby?"

"Gone."

Hunter cursed and the agent handed him a picture. "Agent Crew is aware. He said to give you this."

Hunter took it, slipping out a penlight and shining it onto the photo. Oh, God. It was the baby from Harker's photo album. He closed his eyes. "We'd been so close and now this."

Hunter looked at the man. "Is Crew back?"

"No, sir. Pastori isn't cooperating. He's demanding a lawyer and not talking at all."

Damn, Hunter thought. They had little, if anything on Pastori, only Alice's ID and that he was seen with the other victims. Pastori was the lure and if he didn't finger Harker or Bruiner, they'd have only rape charges to pin on him. The rest was circumstantial.

The agent's handset crackled and Hunter frowned, picking up the police codes. They'd discovered another body, white female, young, a suspected suicide. He put the car in gear.

"Sir, do you think you should go? I mean, your cover."

"I'll risk it."

When they arrived on the scene the place was lit with bright lights and surrounded by yellow tape.

Hunter slipped on a leather jacket, pulling up the collar, then borrowed the agent's FBI ball cap to cover his hair. He walked the perimeter, waiting for forensics to be done, photos to be taken. A forensics officer was kneeling on the ground, casting a footprint. When the signal came, he and one agent moved in to the scene.

Hunter stared down at the young victim. Her wrists were cut clean to the bone, no signs of struggle. According to the coroner, she'd been dead for a few days and had given birth recently. Hunter wanted to tear into something, hit something. She couldn't be more than eighteen.

If she hadn't been cut, she would have died from infection, the coroner told him. Afterbirth was still present.

Hunter scraped his hand over his mouth, a pure unbridled anger slithering through him. They were south of Charleston, nearly to Indigo, but the blood pool had been found much farther north. There was a definite pattern. The east was the shoreline, heavily populated, lots of traffic, even on highway seventeen, which was a long stretch of country road. So that left the west. Hunter looked in that direction, wondering what else he'd find, how many more young women would end up like this.

He's playing with us. He wants the bodies to be found; that's why he dumps them on state property. Hunter needed to find this bastard, right now. Before someone else died.

God, he could barely bring himself to tell Eden.

Impatient for a forensics match between the skin under Helene's nails and the DNA on the coffee cup, Hunter lashed out, demanding the forensics team make it top priority. Girls barely into womanhood were being murdered to the tune of one every two weeks.

"I want everything you have the instant you get it." Hunter pulled out a card and when the guy looked reluctant, he flashed his ID. The man's features tightened and he nodded, taking the card.

Signaling the agent, Hunter climbed into his car and left the scene to the SLED, the FBI and the local police.

WRAPPED IN A SILK ROBE, Eden waited for Hunter. When he came in, she wanted to question him, but then noticed the deep sadness in his eyes. He hadn't shown this much emotion since their project had started.

"Oh, no."

Hunter sat in a chair, then pulled her into his arms, just holding her for a moment.

"Damn, damn," he muttered, and she pressed his head to her chest.

"Please, Hunter, tell me."

He told her about the girl and the Ramsgates, then he told her the truth. "The baby is gone, Eden." He pulled out the photo.

She grabbed it, staring. "It's her! Oh, Lord! What do you mean she's gone?"

"We think Harker took her."

Her breath rushed, her eyes wide. "Oh, my God, she must have used the basket to transport the baby." To have the child so close and now lost broke her heart. "Why would she do that? Why would she kill them?"

"We don't know. The neighbors didn't notice anyone coming or going. It's a busy street."

"How did the FBI find out?"

"There was no movement in the house. Agents looked in the windows and saw them on the floor." Hunter nudged her and she stood. He went to the minifridge and pulled out a beer. Twisting off the cap, he drank half of it before he spoke again. "No basket, no baby, the nanny and the Ramsgates apparently ate poisoned muffins. Mrs. Ramsgate still had a piece in her mouth."

Tears fell, her hands shaking. Then she got angry. "People are dying around us, Hunter! Dying!"

For one brief moment, she struggled to hold it together, but the harder she tried the more she came undone.

Then finally, she shattered. She fell into his arms, her grip almost punishing, and Hunter held on just as tightly, smoothing his hands over her back as she cried. It killed him to hear it. To know he wasn't moving fast enough, learning more that could have saved the Ramsgates.

"All they wanted was a baby to love, and now they're dead."

It was what frightened him about Eden's involvement. "I was angry with you for following Harker, but if you hadn't taken the initiative, no matter how dangerous, we would have never known till the bodies decayed." He nudged her back. "Look at me."

She did and her tear-streaked face sliced him to ribbons.

"You have to be so very careful now, do you understand?"

"Why?"

"You're the only person who can put Harker there at the time of death. If she learns that, she'll try to kill you."

Chapter Thirteen

Hunter couldn't sleep, despite the warm, naked woman beside him. He shifted out of Eden's arms, careful not to wake her. She curled into his pillow, and he twisted to push her hair off her cheek. They'd made slow patient love just a couple of hours ago. Each time since the first, their lovemaking had been more intense, almost strangling him with emotion. Now he pressed his lips to her temple, finally acknowledging the feelings careening though him.

He loved her.

Hell, he'd never fallen out of love with her. He'd simply buried it along with his past, pushed it down deep inside himself where it wouldn't interfere with the life he'd chosen.

Because he *had* chosen it over her.

Now, the choice seemed so unworthy. She meant everything to him. More, perhaps, because they'd both changed so much over the years. He could barely breathe when he thought of being without her.

Yet telling her this was not an option. He didn't deserve more than she'd given him already. He wouldn't assume her forgiveness was any more than her unending compassion. It wasn't a doorway into the future.

And right now, a killer was holding even that hostage till this was over.

She trusted him to find her sister's killer, find the baby, and Hunter felt he'd let her down so far. He couldn't rest, not till he made good his promises.

All of them.

He kissed her once more, then left the bed. He pulled on a pair of cotton drawstring pants, then walked into the living room of the suite, flipping on lights. Gathering his files and the computer, he took them to the sofa.

It was going to be a long night. He wasn't stopping till he had something to work with. He read over each file for the thousandth time, angry that he was missing some idea that would point them in the right direction. Then he opened the computer and with his satellite link, he tapped into files and data no one could without his codes.

He ran a probe program, accessing files he shouldn't—legally. He could lose his position with the CIA for this, but was beyond caring. Everything that meant anything to him was riding on this.

On the screen, Margaret Harker's life spread out before him: her education, her marriage to Walter Harker, now deceased, her training as a midwife.

After an hour of splitting open her life, tracking every license, the purchase of the house, he came across a transaction in her bank account. Pay to the order of Enterprise Estates. A search brought him to a new doorway.

The post-office box had a Summerville, South Carolina zip code, but that wasn't enough. He needed a name. He needed to know where that check had been deposited. He accessed the encrypted files, skirting the state government security measures. He had only minutes before he'd be found out and Hunter's fingers flew over the keyboard as he probed deeper.

Then he was faced with a password. He had three tries. If he got it wrong, it would shut down.

He thought for a moment, then typed her birth date.

Denied Access filled the screen. He went for obscure.

Grandmother.

Denied.

He looked at the pictures of Harker, her smile sweetly serene as she clutched the gold cross hanging from a necklace. He'd bet she thought she was doing the world a great favor, that she was doing God's work. She'd called the babies her angels.

On a hunch, he typed *Savior.* The screen went blank, then blinked up two more consecutive screens. Hunter realized he'd accessed a non-U.S. account in Grand Cayman.

Deposits rolled up the screen.

Jeez, over twenty million.

How long had she been doing this?

He couldn't put an alert on the account. It was the reason the world's finest criminals banked in the islands. Money was nearly untraceable. Well, relatively, he thought, smirking to himself.

He noted the account number and logged off the banking site. He kept working, kept searching, reading over autopsy and forensic files, studying Bruiner's picture.

They had nothing on him, no prints, only a face and suspicion, and Alice's identification. Hunter opened the files on the corporation again, and read the list of shareholders. There were twelve. None of the names were familiar. The screen swam in his visions and dug the heels of his palms in his eyes, then enlarged the print to read the list of company officers. There was only one.

Duke Pastori, CEO.

He leaned his head back on the sofa. *Thank God.*

Thoughts careened in his mind, where to go next, what to do with this, but exhaustion won.

EDEN SMILED down at Hunter. He had the computer on his lap and papers strewn everywhere. He was fast asleep. She straightened the piles, knowing there was a method to his investigation, then peered at the screen.

The computer was still linked to the Internet.

She sat beside him, shifting the warm computer from his lap to hers. She looked around at the files, picking up his notes on Bruiner. Big letters were scribbled across a legal pad. *Who are you?*

So far the man had been untraceable.

Maybe they were looking in the wrong direction?

Eden tried to remember what he'd said about the man. Distinguished, erect posture. She started typing.

Helene was so much better at this, she thought, and felt her sister's presence guiding her. Eden opened window after window, and hit dead ends, not knowing which way to go or what she was really looking for. She glanced at Hunter's notes. He had a couple of pages on real estate, but one scribble caught her interest.

Where are they hiding them?

Hunter's theory had always been that the young mothers were stashed somewhere. Her gaze shifted to the picture of Harris Bruiner. Eden took a wild stab and started a search through local construction companies.

"WHAT ARE YOU DOING?"

Eden flinched, and shot Hunter a startled glance. "I'm helping."

"You could go to jail for accessing CIA files." He rubbed his face, forcing away sleep as he sat up.

She looked at him, her smile tender. "Then trust me with your secrets Hunter. I will keep them."

His lips quirked and he leaned to see what she was searching.

"Besides, these sites are local and public."

"And just what did you find?"

She nudged him. "Don't sound so condescending. I thought about Bruiner, you said he had erect posture and a quick step."

"Yeah. But so do you."

She flashed him a patient look. "Could he be former military?"

"We checked that when we first got the composite."

"But you didn't have a name, only a photo. And he could have had plastic surgery." She waved. "That's not what I was after anyway. I was wondering…if they are hiding these girls and we can't find them, they have to be someplace we wouldn't think to look."

"You have a theory?"

"Charleston is low country, and we're at sea level. No basements, but the bodies were found in the south, one in water, yet the—what did you call it, the kill zone?"

He nodded.

"Well that was north. So, that leaves the west."

"I thought of that."

"Well, west is the Savannah table, where the mountains begin. It's Orangeburg, Aiken. There are hills and horse ranches there, and it's not below sea level. And even if it was, building underground *is* possible."

"If the water table is too low, whatever they did would be flooded in a good hurricane."

"And they would care? You said yourself that you thought they moved around. That doesn't mean they aren't using them now. That's high country. We had a drought last year, Hunter, and not much rain this spring, but that's beside the point." She took a deep breath and declared, "I searched for companies that build survivalist shelters."

Hunter frowned and she shifted the computer toward him. "There aren't any in our area, because they wouldn't be held accountable to the buyer for the water seepage, but what if they told the construction company to go ahead and build?" She tapped the keys and moved the mouse.

It brought up a screen that said Last Man Standing Survivalist Shelters. Built anywhere, any specifications.

"I checked several companies that build shelters within about a two-hundred-mile radius. There were ten, six worked in their areas only, two have gone out of business in the last year, and one moved to Montana. One is still in operation nearby, but I couldn't get any more than an address and what they'll build. It's a company that's been around a long time."

Frowning, Hunter took the computer and started typing. "Who's to say they got a permit, either?" He accessed building-inspector records on the Last Man Standing company. "They've been cited twice for building without a permit." He flicked at the screen. "And they've built some nearer to Columbia."

He looked at her, his smile slow, then he grabbed her close and kissed her soundly. "You're a genius!"

She grinned. "You think it's a good lead?"

"All we need to know is if they've been *here*. And if Enterprise Estate paid them by check."

Hunter looked through the site, estimating the costs from the list shown, then backtracked through Harker's personal bank account. He went back five years and found nothing. He went back seven and found what he was looking for. Esaw Pope. Last Man Standing. A search brought him the address. Another brought him the addresses of Enterprise Estate's properties.

He glanced at the time. "I think we need to wake some people up," he said.

"I'll get ready." Eden kissed his cheek, then headed to the bathroom.

Crew needed to start his morning with something and that Duke Pastori was listed as the CEO of a corporation was just the link they needed.

But it wasn't enough.

Time to call in a favor, he thought. It was the only way he could play this last hunch. He dialed from his computer, skipping the connection across the world, then right back to Langley.

He connected the headset to the computer and waited for the pickup. "Go scramble."

Clicks came over the line. Hunter glanced toward the bedroom when he heard Eden in the shower.

"Code?" the voice said.

Hunter tapped keys.

"Hello, Masked Man," a familiar voice said.

Hunter lips quirked. "I need help."

"I thought you were in-country?"

"I am. I need a search. It isn't sanctioned."

"Since when has that stopped you?"

"Just so you know you're in with both feet from the start, buddy."

The voice on the other end of the line softened. "What do you need?"

"I'm sending you a file, encrypted."

Hunter waited less than a minute before his fellow agent said, "Got it. Handsome devil, isn't he?"

"Can you access facial structure programs?"

"You think he's been rearranged?"

"Yes. We've probed every file we can, except yours."

"I can do it."

"Be discreet. I don't want you to hang for this."

"I'll be sure to pin it on you if I get caught, but I'm sleeping with the analyst."

"Her taste is that bad?"

A soft chuckle came through the line before it went dead.

WHILE HUNTER was somewhere in the west, headed for Last Man Standing, Eden was in the suite, slowly going crazy.

She didn't dare leave till she'd heard from him. Halfway through cleaning up and looking for something to read, she found Hunter's satellite phone tucked in the sofa cushions. At least he had his pager with him, she thought, as she hung up his suit jacket.

It almost hurt to see his things mixed with hers in the closets, and, without thinking about how pathetic it was, she inhaled the scent of his aftershave lingering in the shirt fabric.

She missed him.

She loved him. She wished he'd come back right now so she could tell him. But she wouldn't. If she did, he'd feel obligated to stay, and that would mean giving up his career.

She would never ask that of him.

Moving to the windows, she looked out over the city and prayed Helene's child was somewhere in this town. Somewhere close and safe and not thousands of miles away, as Hunter suspected it might be. The niggling suspicion that Harker had Helene's baby terrified her, because Harker was capable of murder.

The shrill chime of the phone startled her. Hoping it was Hunter, she rushed to answer.

"Hunter?"

"No, dear, this is Margaret."

Eden couldn't have been more stunned. "Oh, hello, Miss Margaret, how are you today?" Eden plastered a false smile on her face and hoped it came through in her voice.

"I have what you want."

"What?"

"A little redheaded baby, right here."

Eden heard the soft gurgling coos of an infant. Hope scavenged through her; she didn't want it to cloud her emotions, but she was a puddle and when the infant made another sweet noise, she thought she'd crumble to the floor.

"Oh, Margaret, really?" she said, trusting she sounded grateful. It wasn't hard not to be honest when she could hear the child and knew it was true.

"Yes. Come get your baby, dear."

"But Hunter isn't here with me right now."

"I'm sure he won't mind if you pick up your child without him. You'll be doing that a lot anyway, won't you?"

Eden frowned, suspicion driving cold fingers up her spine. "Yes, he's a very busy man, but he'll make time for a baby."

"Good. She needs a loving home. Lots of attention. I hate to mention this, but I'll want the fee at the exchange."

"Yes, of course." Eden glanced at the satchel of cash in marked bills. Margaret had stated early on that electronic transfers were not acceptable. She hadn't wanted it to be traceable. Margaret Harker rattled off the address and Eden realized it was the first house where they'd met.

"I'll be there as soon as I can, Miss Margaret."

Eden cut the line, her heartbeat buffeting against the wall of her ribs. The satellite phone was here, and she prayed he carried the one used for the sting. She dialed and got an out-of-range message.

Eden pulled out a change of clothes, then dialed the FBI team.

"Special Agent Crew is on his way back from Alabama, Miss Carlyle, and Officer Couviyon is west of here," the agent told her.

"I know, I need to get a message to both of them, right now." Why did they both have to be out of range now?

She told the agent about Harker's call.

"You cannot meet her alone, ma'am."

"I know it's not smart, so you need to send someone to follow me. Hunter's satellite phone is here. I'll keep it on and with me. But I need to get to that baby, Agent Drescol. I heard the child. She has it."

"She must have taken it from the Ramsgates."

"Probably, but it's an opportunity I can't ignore. Neither would Hunter. We haven't recovered a single child from within the U.S. Harker could take the delay as a lack of interest and do something with the child. Give it away, abandon it, we don't know. Find Hunter. Send someone to the address, please."

"I will. But you have to delay at least fifteen minutes."

"I'll try. Send them now."

She hung up and quickly changed her clothes, grabbed her purse, making certain that Hunter's phone was on and her tazer was charged and ready.

Eden called to the front desk for her car. Within minutes she was headed toward the meeting spot.

She glanced periodically in the rearview mirror, hoping to see an agent.

Hurry, Hunter, please hurry.

Chapter Fourteen

Hunter grabbed on to the strap as the helicopter headed west, toward the last known address of Last Man Standing. The chopper swept over the acreage west of Orangeburg and set down in a small field. The blades were still beating the air when a thin man came out of the squat building, a rifle slung in his arms like a baby.

Hunter left the chopper with four agents and hurried toward the man.

He aimed his rifle. "Not another step."

"FBI." They flashed badges and aimed weapons. The man didn't blink.

"I don't care if you're the damn president, get off my land."

"Sir, we're here to talk," the agent in charge said.

Out of patience, Hunter started walking. The man shouldered the rifle, aiming. Hunter leaped forward, snatching the barrel. The round fired into the air.

Instantly, the man was surrounded and disarmed.

Hunter stopped them shy of cuffing him. "You should have known when to back off yourself, Mr. Pope," Hunter said.

Esaw Pope was a rangy man with a bald scalp so tanned and wrinkled it looked as if it would slide into his eyes any second. He wore a military surplus camouflage uniform.

"We need to see your plans for shelters. All your records."

"Hell, no." When Pope turned and walked into his little house as if that was that, Hunter followed.

"Hey, I didn't invite you in!"

"After that show, I don't need an invitation."

The FBI agents filed in with him, each man noticing the arsenal of weapons racked in every corner of the house. Agents strolled, not touching anything but writing down the serial numbers. Hunter counted three illegal machine guns.

"Get the hell outta my house."

"Sir, we are here to ask questions and nothing more," an agent said.

"I'm not answering a single one, so you might as well git along right now."

Hunter stepped forward. "Gentlemen," he said in a calm voice, his gaze locked on Pope. "Why don't you give me a few minutes alone with Mr. Pope?"

Pope looked at the other agents, panic skating across his features before he shored up his defenses.

Hunter didn't move, his hands shoved deep in his pockets. Slowly, the other men filed out.

Pope looked around, his gaze falling on the nearest weapon.

"That wouldn't be smart." Hunter opened his coat slightly to show his weapon.

"A man has a right to protect his property."

"Yes, he does. But it's not your property you should be worried about." He stared, knowing what he looked like, knowing how effective it was. Hunter didn't have the time to waste. And he wasn't leaving empty-handed.

He moved in close, crowding Pope. The man's gaze shot around for an exit. Hunter wasn't offering one. He towered over him by eight inches, and though he kept his hands casual, Esaw Pope wasn't getting past him.

"I'm not like those guys," Hunter said softly, inclining his head to the agents outside. "I'm with the company, you understand?"

Hunter knew he did when the man's eyes narrowed.

Esaw spat a sour look. "As if I care? You're all leading us to nuclear war." Pope started to shove him, then thought better of it and lowered his hands.

Hunter arched a brow. "You *should* care. I don't have many laws that hold me back."

"You can't hurt me."

"I can. I will."

Sweat beaded on Pope's upper lip.

"Let me make myself clear. You build underground shelters. People have used those shelters to keep innocent young and very pregnant girls hostage. They've been murdered. Six so far."

"I didn't have nuthin' to do with that!"

"Yes, you did. You gave them a place to hide those girls."

"A man's business is his own. I got rights."

"Not today." In a heartbeat Hunter was on him, his fist wrapped in Pope's clothes, shoving him up against the wall. Framed pictures flopped, then fell.

No one came in.

"People have died, people could be dying now. You have a daughter, Esaw? You have a grandchild?" Hunter knew, he'd seen pictures all over the house between the cache of weapons.

The man nodded.

"Well, some man's grandchild's been sold on the black market. American babies. Some man's daughter's been cut up in the woods and left for the animals."

"I didn't know! I swear! I swear I'd never be part of that!"

"Good, good," Hunter said calmly, then stepped back, releasing Pope. "Are you ready to cooperate?"

Esaw nodded, his skinny body going limp, his eyes round as he choked for air. The man struggled to reach for a chair, then sagged into it, cupping his head in his hands. Hunter called to the other agents.

"Mr. Pope is willing to help us, gentleman. Isn't that right, Mr. Pope?"

Pope nodded almost violently.

"I want to know where you built the shelters, exactly. I want the plans, the locations and anything else you might have."

Esaw sent him a nasty look, stood, then walked stiffly across the room and out a door. Hunter was on him, weapon drawn, the other agents turning as he moved. Pope walked to a little shack out behind the house. It had one door, no windows. Pope threw his shoulder into the door, and pushed it open. Hunter could hear the suction of a tight seal.

While the yard looked more like a military command post, the little office resembled a fifties bomb shelter. It led downward and Pope stopped at a file cabinet at the base of wood steps. He opened a drawer.

"You know when it was built?"

"No."

"Jeez, I've been building shelters for fifteen years." Pope flicked though the folders in the back of the drawer.

"It might have been a woman, a little old lady."

Pope's head jerked up, his gaze thinning as he said, "Yeah, I remember her."

He went right to the file and handed it over.

Hunter flipped it open, scanned it. His gaze snapped to Pope's. "You built more than one for her?"

OVER THE CHOPPER RADIO, Hunter pressed the head phones tighter and listened to Crew.

"I got your fax about Enterprise Estates and the copy of the boot print. Pastori copped a plea. He didn't know he was listed as the CEO. He insists he didn't know the company existed. Nor did he realize his boots could be identified. It's a match down to the worn right heel. The arrogant cuss put them on the desk, in clear view, God love the idiot. He still had dirt in them, with traces of blood that put him at Maddy Beasely's murder."

"Did he give up any more?"

"You don't want much do you, Couviyon? Yeah, he said Harris Bruiner killed them. Though Pastori said he never let him see it. Bruiner stripped down to his skin, covered his hands and his feet with latex gloves and bags, and he shaved his body."

"Premeditated."

Crew agreed.

"And he's bald."

Hunter scowled. "I saw him with dark hair."

"A wig, top of the line, like they use in movies."

"No wonder the agents didn't see him leaving the mall."

"Pastori carted the bodies to the drop-off. He said they just drove till they hit a certain mile count and dropped them."

"So all the evidence would point to Pastori."

"He wasn't going to jail for Bruiner, he said. That's what clinched it for him. He realized he was being set up to take the rap for the murders."

Hunter didn't give a crap what Pastori thought. He

was a rapist and an accessory to murders and kidnapping. He hoped he got the death penalty. "What was the method?"

"He was paid thirty grand to find the girls. He used the clinic kid to get the information, then presented himself to the girls. He admitted that some weren't pregnant before he got a hold of them. Some of the girls came from the streets, others were runaways."

Hunter made a disgusted face. "Takes all kinds."

"Pastori took care of them, they lived with him, one at a time. With each girl it was a new apartment, or house. Everything that was in the apartments was destroyed or sold before Pastori moved on to another apartment."

"Well, there's the reason we couldn't find an address or anything belonging to the victims." The only items Eden had were what Helene's former roommate had kept. The invitation to the charity ball must have been a bribe by Bruiner, implying money and power to the frightened, isolated girl. Bruiner had never intended for Helene to go to the party.

"Some were sublets, some were house-sitting in summer homes on Isle of Palms. I have several addresses to check. Going to be a nightmare for the forensics, especially with the summer cottages used by several families all year long. It will take weeks just to go through it all and gather information."

"So when the girls reached term he drugged them and brought them to Bruiner?"

"Yes. He insists that was the end of his part."

"My ass it was," Hunter snapped. "He was there when they were killed. He drove them, he carried them from the kill zone. That boot print proves it. Did he rape them, Crew?"

"He admitted to raping the girl in Alabama, but not the others. DNA matching on the babies will tell us something."

"We have to find them first. We have nothing on the bug in Harker's place."

"Sir," an agent across from him interrupted. "Forensics has a match." He gestured to his cell phone. "DNA from the coffee cup matches with the skin found under Helene Carlyle's fingernails."

Hunter relayed the information to Crew. "We have our killer."

EDEN CIRCLED THE BLOCK, her attention flitting to the house as she tried to maneuver in traffic. She waited an extra five minutes, and when her cell rang with the FBI agent saying they were two blocks away, she let out a relieved breath and felt safer.

But when Margaret stepped out on the porch with the baby in her arms, Eden knew there was no more time. The woman spotted her and waved. Eden smiled brightly and had no choice but to pull into the driveway. Harker stepped off the porch, walking toward her.

Her gaze on the bundle in Harker's arms, Eden pushed on the car door latch, but the door wouldn't budge.

She jerked on the handle, then shoved with her shoulder.

The door shoved back.

She looked up, and staring down at her was the man from the composite.

Harris Bruiner.

She scrambled away from him, reaching for the tazer and got the satellite phone. She pressed Send.

It was the last thing she did before pain exploded in the back of her skull.

DUSK PAINTED THE SKY. Inside the chopper heading toward Charleston, Hunter was coordinating a search for the shelters when his pocket hummed. Patting himself down for the satellite phone, he groaned when he realized he had only the cell phone under the name Lockwood he'd given Harker. He swore and the image of the sofa in the suite popped in his mind. Hunter dialed the first message and heard Eden's voice, excited and a little scared.

"Harker has the child. I'm meeting her at the first house. I've called the FBI, and they're sending someone to follow me."

Panic such as he'd never known swept through him and started eating at his insides. He shouted at the pilot to head toward Harker's address, then radioed Crew before he listened to the next message from his satellite phone. He heard a man's voice, Harker's in the background. Then a soft popping sound that was all too familiar.

Silencer-enhanced gunfire. Oh, God.

"Put it on the ground!" Hunter stared out the window as the chopper began its descent. A block away a black sedan was smashed into a parked car, a man slumped over the steering wheel. Even at this distance Hunter could see that the back of his skull was blown out. In Harker's driveway, Eden's car sat empty, the door open.

The helicopter barely touched down before Hunter was out and running, agents spilling from the steel cavity behind him. SLED surrounded the house, FBI kicking in the door. But even before he entered, he knew she'd be gone.

Holstering his weapon, Hunter moved back outside to the car. Her handbag was still inside with the tazer.

Blood smears darkened the seat. Hunter thought his legs would give out under him and he forced himself to think, to know his next move and be certain it was the right one.

Crowding his mind was Eden, hurt, defenseless, in the hands of a killer. And it was his fault.

A car sped to a halt near the commotion and Crew climbed out. "We found an agent a block away—"

"He's dead, I saw it from the air."

"One shot through the head. A couple of kids heard the crash, but didn't see anyone, just a black van speeding away."

Hunter mashed a hand over his face. A silencer hit, at long range. Bruiner had killed over a dozen times, why spare Eden? To what end?

"Isn't this Eden's car?" Crew said, peering inside.

"They have her. And the child."

And Hunter had the locations of the shelters. They had been built years ago and Pope didn't keep good records, but being a militiaman, he kept excellent maps.

Hunter was walking away from the car when he heard a tone and recognizing it, he turned back. His satellite phone was on the floorboards. He grabbed it, and looked at the number before answering. Langley. CIA. "Tell me I was right, pal."

"You were. We made him. He was one of us."

Hunter pinched the bridge of his nose.

"More specifically, Masked Man, he's one of *you.*"

EDEN FELT THE UNEVEN road radiate up through the tires, vibrating the steel frame of the van. The hollow tinny sound battered against her skull, turning the pain from aching to numbing.

The FBI agent who was tailing her was dead, or he would have stopped them. It made her sick to think of how many had died already. She wasn't planning on being the next.

She forced her eyes open, squinting. She was in the back of a dark van on a mattress that reeked of age and ill use. Her gaze focused on the front: a hooded driver and passengers. She wasn't all that startled to see Margaret Harker sitting comfortably in a second row captain's seat—cuddling a swaddled bundle in her arms.

The baby.

She tried to move, and realized her arms were restrained. Someone sat nearby, silent and staring. Turning her head, her gaze rose to the face cloaked in shadows, but there was no mistaking Harris Bruiner.

The green glow from the dashboard lights painted the van's ceiling, showering down on his handsome features with a ghoulish glow, making his face appear suspended in a river of black.

He looked comfortable sitting in the rear, unruffled by the circumstances. He'd done it before, several times, why would this be any different? His gaze moved over her, pausing on her hair, and the lifted corner of his mouth hinted at his pleasure.

Redheads. All the victims had been redheads.

She looked at Harker. "You're mad if you think you can get away with his." The threat was empty, useless.

Margaret merely smiled, adjusting the baby in her arms. Eden saw tiny legs kicking for a second before Harker covered them from the cold.

"Isn't she lovely?"

Eden knew nothing right then but a hunger to see the child, to hold her. She wanted the only part of her sister left locked in her arms. And safely away from these monsters.

Harker adjusted the child so Eden could see her

face. *She looks just like Helene did.* Eden said prayer on top of prayer that she would help this child grow to womanhood. That Hunter was as smart as she thought and would find her soon.

One look at Bruiner told Eden she didn't have much time. He was like a teen anticipating his first back-seat drive-in. She could almost smell it on him, the destructive hunger to kill. Her stomach rolled loosely and she swallowed.

"Did you think I wouldn't know you put the bug in my office?" Harker said. "You and Hunter were the only ones in there in weeks and my people sweep the place for things like that after each client."

Eden didn't care how they found out. Her only concern was her life and that baby. "What are you going to do with the baby?"

Harker scoffed. "Nothing. She'll be well cared for, given to parents who want her and will keep her in the lap of luxury. Not like your sister. You look just like her. I knew why you wanted this particular baby, Eden. I've been doing this a long time."

"Murdering innocent girls?" Pain in her head made her slur her words.

"They weren't innocent, they were whores, getting themselves pregnant like that."

Eden's gaze swung purposely to Bruiner. "I'm sure they had help."

Bruiner's upper lip curled, the only show of the emotions locked behind a dark stare.

"Please don't hurt her."

"I would never harm the child," Harker snapped. "Never. They've grown up with wealth and privilege instead of in poverty."

"You don't know they would have lived like that."

"Yes, I do." Harker's gaze flashed to her left. "Isn't that right, Raymond?"

Raymond? Eden's gaze flicked. Harris Bruiner was an alias. Of course. Eden rose up as best she could, struggling to touch her sister's child. Just once. Harker angled the child away, and Eden's heart broke into a million pieces, floating away as Harker nodded.

To Bruiner.

He pushed her down, making her head smack against the iron edge of the bed. Eden bit down on her lip, wishing she could do something to help herself. Wishing for the skill and strength to hit Bruiner, Harker, even cause an accident...but she wouldn't endanger the baby.

And they knew it.

She felt a prick in her arm and looked. Bruiner was sliding a needle out, the syringe empty.

Then, so was her mind.

Chapter Fifteen

With five choppers in the air sweeping for the black van, Hunter was at least thirty minutes behind the kidnappers. Thirty minutes farther from Eden.

Fear devoured him from the inside. Eden was in the hands of a serial killer, and they knew they'd been set up. They were out of time. Out of options. The only thing in his favor was Esaw Pope and his maps.

If Hunter didn't move fast, Eden would share a plot with her sister. The thought clawed at his heart as the chopper swooped over the city like a winged falcon chasing down its prey. Hunter was in the co-pilot seat, adjusting the headset.

"Bruiner's mine, you got that?"

"Couviyon."

"No, Crew. Don't throw jurisdiction at me now. We made him."

Crew frowned, pressing the headset to his ear.

"We—the CIA—we made him. He was reported dead, under thirty feet of rubble in Libya, yet he's here."

Hunter had waited long enough to hear the dossier on Harris Bruiner from his CIA contact. He relayed it to Crew. All of it. Harris Bruiner, aka Harry Dovin, aka Ray Spicer, had been in the navy, a corpsman. He'd been charged with assaulting a female sailor, the charges dropped. A day later he was assigned as a field medic, then recruited for a CIA operation. From then on, he was theirs. There was suspicion of unsanctioned kills and that he was a sexual predator. His navy medic training meant he knew how to drug his targets, how to use IVs and needles. While the CIA had made him a ghost.

"We couldn't find him because he's had considerable plastic surgery and has no prints. They were surgically removed." Crew looked at him in disgust and Hunter wiggled his fingers. "Yes, I have mine." Bruiner had worn gloves so he wouldn't leave behind any DNA. Hunter turned the computer toward Crew and the picture came up. "That's what he looked like before."

Crew leaned forward. "Ugly sucker."

"He was chosen to blend in, to attract no attention. Before he reemerged, he'd altered himself to look more appealing to his targets. This is a career killer, and he's skilled at evasion."

While they spoke, agents checked their weapons, loaded tear gas launchers.

Hunter turned up the maps, pointing. "This is where Pope said he built the second shelter. The first is here."

"Then why are we headed in the other direction?"

"The first is closer to Charleston. I'm betting they keep the babies there." Harker's residence had turned up nothing to implicate her. The minute he'd learned about the two shelters from Pope, Hunter had sent a team to the first site.

"That's a big hunch you're playing, Hunter."

"We don't have much choice, they're too far apart and we're short on time."

"If we're wrong, it could cost Eden her life."

Hunter's features tightened. He didn't have to be reminded. If he failed, Eden would die—tonight.

ODORS STUNG her nostrils, a sickening combination of dank mustiness that reeked of mildew and old dirt. For a split second, Eden imagined she was buried underground.

It smelled like an open grave.

The edges of her mind were hazy, her head pounding so hard she couldn't open her eyes beyond slits. For her own safety, she remained still. She'd no sense of time, no sense of walls or ceiling. Her body floated. Noise was almost nonexistent.

She struggled to push aside the foggy cloud in her mind and a single memory flickered to life: being carried down into darkness, the jolt of each footstep vibrating up her body to her head. She'd just wanted it to end. But it hadn't.

In the edges of her hearing the sound of metal against metal filtered in. *Open your eyes.*

Open your eyes, she told herself.

She did, her lids sluggish, heavy.

Above her was a single bulb, glaring and stark. She tried moving her head and couldn't. Her skull was strapped down to a hard bed. Her ankles were shackled. She felt something pull at the skin on her arm, and her gaze circled till it landed on the IV bag hanging from a silver rod.

She scanned her circumference. There was a woman beside her on her right, heavily pregnant. All Eden could see was her distended belly and dirty bare feet. To her left was nothing but blackness. Near her feet and to the right was another woman, also about to deliver. She gripped her belly and moved like a zombie. Her hair was dirty and her soiled and wrinkled clothing torn and out of style. She moved without direction, each troubled step accompanied with the scrap.

She's chained like a dog.

Her gaze shifted to the far left at her feet. She felt a presence, someone hovering in the darkened corner like a wolf about to strike. She knew it was Bruiner.

And terror swept her. He'd killed her sister, tried to kill Alice. He'd murdered Maddy Beasely only a few days ago.

A creak came, sounding like the hinge of a door, and then Harker appeared, childless and at her side.

"Too bad you're not pregnant, too."

Her bony hand smoothed over Eden's abdomen

and the urge to vomit made her mouth water. *Go to hell!* she wanted to yell, but her lips wouldn't move. Her expression amused Harker.

Harker flicked a hand toward the wall and Bruiner moved forward. Out of the shadows. Even in the small room, Eden heard the other women move away, saw one cower and make a sound that was pure fear and hatred.

Her gaze locked on Bruiner, and she understood why women were attracted to him. Wanted him. He was no less handsome than Hunter; tall and built, his jaw was a chiseled cut of flesh and bone, his deep-set eyes mysteriously brown.

There was no warmth in them. Not a shred.

His black leather jacket creaked as he lifted his arms, one hand grasping the IV tube, the other holding a loaded syringe. He injected red liquid into the reservoir. Eden saw the tube turn pink, the slow flow toward her veins. Her hearing lessened, her shoulders and neck numbed.

All the things she hadn't done, hadn't said, skipped through her mind.

Hunter. I love you.

Then she knew.

She was dying.

ACCESS ROADS were blocked, choppers were in the air or landing with medical teams standing by. Hunter and Aidan Crew moved into the forest, bypassing the fire roads. Behind them at the edge of the forest were the horses they'd ridden. Creeks and ravines laced this part of the state; traversing them on foot a waste of time they didn't have. Minutes counted.

Seconds did.

Hunter swallowed, forcing himself to focus and making himself forget that he'd spent years doing this sort of thing instead of lying in Eden's arms. That he'd failed her again and hadn't told her he loved her. The only thing in their favor was that neither Harker nor Bruiner were aware they'd discovered the shelters. Hunter owed that to Eden.

Beside Hunter, a few feet to his right, was Aiken's county deputy sheriff. His men had spotted the van tracks, pinpointing the last location. Hunter appreciated men who knew their own backyard.

The deputy sheriff tapped him, and Hunter looked to his right, then he saw it. The small flash of metal in a forest of green. They moved in, circling the area before coming closer. The setting sun glinted off something else.

Hunter touched the mike at his throat and said, "Everyone, stop. Look down. The place is wired."

He followed a line of trip wire to a tree. The sheriff inched closer, his eyes wide. Carefully, Hunter spread the branches and leaves covering the device. There were enough explosives to take down the tree and drop it on whoever was near.

"Can you disarm that thing?"

Hunter nodded, kneeling slowly. Wires went out

in three directions. Linked, no doubt, to more. He pulled out a Swiss Army knife he'd carried since he was sixteen. The multitool had saved his butt a hundred times in the last seven years. He snapped out the screwdriver to remove the device's casing, then the wire cutters. He clipped the wires, disarming the charges, then motioned the sheriff and Crew to step over it. Hunter followed the wire to the next one, making certain the charges were disabled from the pins. One was designed to set off a series of them. Once Hunter located the free zone to walk through, it led right to a clearing.

Hunter touched the throat mike, raising Crew. "Pope said he'd disguised it. It's been several years. It won't be recognizable."

"It's your game, Couviyon, your call."

Hunter nodded, his expression suppressing his fear. He'd never failed an assignment before. He sure as hell wasn't going to fail now.

The clearing was minimal, the tracks leading into a curtain of vines. Hunter approached first, Crew several steps behind him. Hunter warned the others to look down. No telling what Bruiner had concocted to keep people out or to alert him to intruders.

Hunter pushed at the vines and dry pine boughs. The light had reflected off the corner of the wheel hub of the van. He peered inside, then moved under the swath of green and greeted pitch-black darkness. A tin frame covered the van like a carport. Hunter flicked on a penlight, his steps quiet as Crew followed behind. A single thick door lay in their path, tilted into a mound of earth.

"It must go downward," Hunter whispered. "I don't think my tools are going to get us in, and we have to have the element of surprise."

Crew muscled his way past him and Hunter grinned as the agent whipped out a lock pick. "Sure you're with the right organization, Aiden?"

Crew smirked, and the door lock gave. No alarms went off, unless there were silent alarms.

Hunter stood on the threshold, inky darkness on the other side. He didn't know if the ground dropped out from under him or went flat. He felt for a switch on the wall. Nodding to Crew, he flipped it.

Several yards away was a wall, the upper half glass like a hospital viewing ward. Beyond it were cribs. A dozen at least. It was like a factory. He scanned the room for cameras and alarms, then touched the mike. "We're in, and be careful. There are cribs in here." He didn't hear any noises from the cribs, didn't see any babies.

Hunter hung back. Crew moved to the two doors they could see. Crew inclined his head. Hunter shook his.

This couldn't be the only way in. Crew scowled till Hunter signaled that he was going outside to look for another entrance and needed two minutes. Nodding, Crew positioned himself and his team at the door as Hunter backed out of the underground building, then hurried along the edge, moving out to the north. The sun was nearly down, the woods turning dark with the moonless sky. The land was sparse. He stepped slowly, listening to his own feet on the ground. He didn't think that Helene or Alice had escaped on their own, but that they were out in the open when they broke free.

Bruiner was smart. He'd make it impossible for drugged girls to get out. Yet no operative went into a fortress without an escape route. Hunter was counting on that. He signaled the deputies to move toward him. Hunter walked slightly left, then right.

That's when he felt the earth give beneath his boot. Hollow and less dense. Wood. Kneeling, he swept aside pine needles and leaves and found a hatch, broad and thick. Scrape marks marred the ground. There was blood on the handle. Silently signaling the others to remain above, Hunter reached for the metal latch.

HE STARED DOWN AT HER. He'd known who she was when he'd seen her sitting in the car. The sister. Helene had spoken about her often. He'd convinced Helene not to contact her. That she didn't care or she would have come before now. Helene hadn't known that he'd rerouted her calls, that he'd destroyed her letters. He'd even taken her on a trip north to keep her from contacting her sister. She didn't want to or she would have tried harder, Helene had not been a stupid woman. He touched Eden's face, seeing the other.

You came for the baby, didn't you, Eden?

Well, like your sister, you won't get it.

He fingered a curl of hair the color of polished copper, seeing another, a woman who'd whored with men but never loved them. Who'd bred babies she'd never wanted. Mothers. They didn't deserve the name. But he'd taken care of that.

THE CINDER-BLOCK tunnel was narrow enough that Hunter's shoulders scraped the wall. Behind him was a ten-foot drop from the surface, the ladder short and tilted straight up. Ahead, a string of lights paved the way into the shelter.

Hunter came to a fork in the corridor, listened, then followed the sounds. Light glowed a short distance away, and he hovered back, out of sight. The walls were reinforced with cinder blocks and steel, covered in places with plasterboard. There was a small kitchen on the far wall, and glass cabinets of medical equipment lining the right, a birthing table in the center of a tiled floor. There was a drain in the middle, under the table.

Less than ten yards from him, Margaret Harker sat at a table, eating a sandwich, sipping tea. She checked her watch twice in the space of a minute. Beyond and over her head he could see the staircase leading upward. Crew was on the other side. Hunter checked his watch, his two-minute favor was nearly up. The one advantage they had was that the shelter was not directly under the building, so sound wouldn't travel so easily. Then it did, a scraping noise.

Slowly, Harker set down her cup as she looked back over her shoulder, then she wiped her mouth before going to investigate. She mounted the staircase.

Hunter backed up into the tunnel and turned sharply right. He came to a dead stop before a steel-reinforced door. He reached for the knob.

"I was expecting you," a voice said from behind.

Hunter went still, feeling the cold press of a knife to his jugular.

"Arms up, drop the gun."

Hunter obeyed. The pistol dropped to the dirt floor.

"You're too late," the voice said. "She's dead already."

Hunter closed his eyes against the rage rushing through his blood. He refused to believe that. "Then you die tonight, too."

Bruiner scoffed. "Move." He pushed the knife, pricking Hunter's skin.

Hunter walked from the corridor to the room, all the while scanning the area for a weapon. "It's over, you know."

"I haven't lasted this long without knowing how to get out. Turn around."

Hunter did, the knife point scraping along his throat as he turned and came face to face with Harris Bruiner.

He could almost smell the insanity bottled inside

him. It permeated his skin like a foul vapor passing through his expensive black silk shirt. *We helped create this creature,* Hunter thought, staring into empty eyes.

This time, Bruiner was bald.

"You should run." Hunter shifted right, putting his back to a wall. "Or didn't you notice that Harker didn't come back?"

"Margaret made her bed, now she lies in it."

Bruiner took a swipe and Hunter lurched back, watching his hands, knowing they'd had the same training. But Bruiner had the death penalty lingering over him right now. That made him more dangerous.

Hunter wanted him to be careless.

"Your mother was a redhead." They circled each other, Bruiner waving the knife, hoping to get Hunter to follow it. He wouldn't.

Bruiner's expression went even flatter. "She wasn't my mother, she was a whore." His dull tone belied the energy unleashing in him and Bruiner struck, cutting through Hunter's jacket and into his arm. Hunter let it bleed, his fist shooting out and knocking Bruiner's head back. Blood trickled from his nose.

The room erupted with FBI agents suddenly, yet neither man's attention veered from the other. No less than a dozen assault rifles were cocked and aimed.

"Don't shoot. He's mine!" Hunter said. "Crew, in the back, hurry. Eden's in there."

Crew rushed past to the door.

Bruiner's glaze flicked to the armed men. "Why don't you just kill me?" He swiped at his nose, resolute. He still held the knife.

"That would be too easy." Fists primed, Hunter punched, not aiming for Bruiner's face, but his wrist. Contact sent the blade flying across the room. "You'll stand trial. You'll die while their loved ones watch." A second blow to the throat drove Bruiner back against the exam table, gasping. A tray of instruments scattered and spilled. Bruiner pushed off and attacked, brandishing a scalpel.

He lunged, impotent rage contorting his features. Hunter caught the man's hand; Bruiner aimed for the artery, driving them back against the wall. Dirt dusted them.

"I watched them die, like your woman," Bruiner taunted, fighting to put the blade in Hunter's jugular. "It was a beautiful death."

Driven by madness, Bruiner's strength was ungodly, and Hunter struggled to keep the blade from his throat. One stab to the jugular and he'd bleed to death in seconds. He wasn't giving up.

He fought for the young girls who'd never have a future or hold their babies. He fought for Eden and gained strength. The more Bruiner tried to push the knife into his throat, the harder Hunter pushed back.

Then Bruiner's wrist snapped. Bone punched through the skin. The scalpel tumbled and Bruiner howled, clutching his ruined arm, staggering.

"Hunter!" Crew shouted. "I've got the door open!"

Hunter executed a roundhouse kick that connected with Bruiner's jaw. He went down and Hunter didn't look back as he rushed to the other room.

Crew crashed through the door, Hunter behind him.

It was dank and wet. Four women lay on flatbeds, the last was Eden. Hunter rushed to her side, touching her face. She was cold. His heart exploded, his fear realized. He touched her throat, and couldn't feel a pulse. He removed her bonds and the IV, calling her name. That's when he saw the IV tubing crushed and bent in her hand.

He tried to rouse her as emergency medical technicians entered the cavern. Then he found her pulse, weak and slowing. Hunter scooped her into his arms, shouldering his way past agents and police, carrying her from the shelter and out into the night. The choppers were landing in the nearby field and Hunter couldn't wait.

He ran, begging God.

The doors flung open and he climbed in, laying Eden on the stretcher. The chopper lifted off instantly.

"Eden, baby, wake up. Please, honey." His eyes burned. Jesus, not like this. *Not like this.* He tapped her face, rubbed her wrists. Opposite him an EMT worked like mad to revive her. "Look at me, honey, look at me." He peeled open her eyes. They swam in her head. "Eden!"

The EMT glanced up, his eyes so sad Hunter felt himself split apart.

"No! She's not dead." She'd bent the tube to keep the drugs from getting in her. It told him she wasn't giving up. He wouldn't accept that she would now.

The EMT kept working and Hunter pressed his lips to Eden's temple as the chopper sped toward the hospital.

"Don't die, fight!" he whispered in her ear. "I haven't had the chance to love you enough yet."

Chapter Sixteen

In the hospital, Eden stirred from a soft, restful place, her eyes slowly adjusting to the darkened room. Sunlight streamed through the blinds down over Hunter. He was asleep in the chair, his head on the edge of the mattress. She shifted to her side, wincing a little, then touched his hair.

His head snapped up and he blinked. His smile was slow, spreading across his face, lighting his eyes. "Hi."

"Hi, yourself." Her fingertips skittered over his face as he crawled onto the bed and gathered her in his arms.

For a long moment, he simply held her. "You scared the hell out of me, woman."

Eden felt him tremble. "I know. I'm sorry." Oh, it felt so good to be right here in his arms again.

He leaned back, his gaze searching her face. "You saved your own life by bending that tube. The drugs would have killed you." His voice fractured a little, his eyes going glossy.

She pushed a lock of his hair back, touched his face. "He never said a word, not a single word." Her lip trembled and he kissed it away.

"He's behind bars." She fingered his bloodstained shirt, then eyed him. "Just a scratch."

"The other women?"

"They each delivered within hours. They'll be better in a few days." He kissed her forehead, her mouth.

She pushed him back. "You're not saying it, Hunter. You didn't find Helene's child, did you?" He shook his head, and she fell back into the pillows. "I should have expected it, I guess."

She stared blankly at the windows, hurting down to her soul.

"Harker's being questioned still. It's not over."

Someone knocked, then Agent Crew stuck his head in. Eden forced a smile. He winked at her, then looked at Hunter. "Get your rubber hose, because you get a crack at Harker."

Hunter nodded and as Crew slipped out, he looked at Eden. She toyed with the sheets on her lap.

"Go do what you must, Hunter." Her throat was so tight she could barely speak. "I'll be fine."

"Hey, hey, look at me." She did, and her sorrow was so tangible, he felt it like a stabbing wound.

"You have a job to finish, and I know you, you won't stop until it's done."

"I won't let you down, Eden. I love you."

She blinked.

"I didn't think I'd ever get the chance to say that."

"So you thought you'd just throw that out there and see what happens?"

His expression was full of hope. "*Is* anything happening?"

Oh, this shouldn't hurt so much again, she thought, and all she could do was nod.

He tipped her chin, his gaze locked on her. "I love you, Eden. You've been mine for years, and that will never change."

She couldn't give her heart up by speaking the words. Not when everything felt so uncertain. "But you aren't going to be here, so where does that leave me?"

"I'll come back."

"When? For how long?"

"I don't know yet, you just have to trust me."

She arched a brow.

"Please?"

She nodded and he kissed her softly, then left her, alone.

THE MINUTE she was released from the hospital, Eden went home. She left everything behind but her car, wanting to banish the past days from her mind and Hunter from her heart. It was a hopeless wish. He was there, buried so deep in her heart she could scarcely breathe when she thought of him. But in the past days she'd heard nothing.

No news. No Hunter. No baby. Agent Crew had

at least called to say the second shelter had held records of babies going back forty years, that Harker's daughters, who'd taken care of the infants, had plea-bargained for leniency if they disclosed the entire truth. But no, they hadn't found Helene's baby.

Her back against a short stone wall on the waterfront, Eden glanced back at her café. The minute the news of the black-market ring had broken, and her involvement, Indigo was a hot spot, her café the main attraction.

People strolled past, barely noticing her sitting on the ground when there were benches lining the walk. She looked out over the water, drawing up her legs, and wrapping her arms around her knees.

It was Hunter's family she'd had a hard time with, though. Looking them in the eye and not telling them she'd been with Hunter all this time felt like betrayal. But he'd asked her not to say anything and she'd agreed. What did it matter? She was in love with him again and he was gone, vanished. Just like last time. Eden's throat tightened, and she bowed her head, her forehead on her knees.

"Eden."

Her head jerked up and she shielded her eyes against the sun. Her breath left in one hard push. She couldn't move. Hunter stood a few feet away, his handsome face somber. Then he walked close, kneeling. His gaze shifted wildly over her face.

"Where have you been?" she said, her voice fracturing.

"Righting some wrongs." He grasped her hand, pulling her from the ground. "I want to come home, Eden."

"It looks like you are already."

She wasn't giving him an inch, but he'd expected that. "Not just to Indigo, but to you."

Her breath caught. "Are you sure?"

"More than I've been about anything."

"You're giving up your career?" She shook her head. "I can't let you. I won't."

"You don't have a choice. It's done." Later he would tell her he'd joined the FBI, working with his new partner, Aidan Crew.

"But, Hunter—"

He gripped her arms, hauling her close. "My God, you're still so damn stubborn. Don't you understand? I love you!" He gazed deep into eyes that haunted his dreams. "Nothing like I did seven years ago. This is different. This is stronger. You know that."

Her eyes teared, her silence tearing him apart.

"I went through hell to find my feelings again, Eden. Even risking all I did for seven years, not one moment was wasted, because it brought me back where I belong. To you. I love you," he said fiercely. "So much I can't live another moment without you. I won't."

Eden stared up at him, the truth and his pledge were in his eyes.

Fear laced his voice when he said, "Can you give me a second chance?"

Stripped and humble, he laid his heart in her hands, waiting for her to gather him close or turn him away. Eden couldn't ask for more. She didn't need it.

Her smile sent quiet tears spilling down her cheeks. "Oh, Hunter. Yes. I love you so much." She touched his jaw, his lips. "I was afraid if I told you, you'd feel obligated to stay. And I didn't want you like that, I never did."

Hunter let out a long breath, pressing his forehead to hers and feeling the freedom of her love sweep through him. "You were never an obligation, ever." He kissed her softly, languidly, then dipped his hand into his pocket and pulled it out, holding a diamond ring between his thumb and forefinger. "I think this one is more your taste."

She inhaled, her gaze snapping to his.

"Will you marry me? Make a home and babies with me?"

Her smile faltered a little. She stared at the ring, then him. New starts, she thought. New beginnings. "Yes, I will."

He slid the ring on her finger, then drew her into his arms, kissing her deeply, uncaring of the passersby—only of the woman in his arms and the happiness she gave him.

Before their kiss got out of hand, he drew back. "I'll just be a second."

"Leaving already?"

"Never." He kissed her, quick and wild, then .

crossed the grounds and disappeared around the edge of the building. Eden was studying her diamond ring when he called to her.

She looked up. Logan, Nash and Temple walked beside Hunter, yet her gaze landed on the bundle of pink in Hunter's arms. Eden rushed to him, covering her mouth for a second as her gaze flicked from his face to the bundle. Her heart jumped as he pushed back the blanket.

A tuft of red hair shone like a beacon.

She choked, sobbing, as he laid the baby in her arms, and Eden clutched the child close, then folded to the ground, crying. Hunter knelt, wrapping his arms around her, feeling his heart take flight and soar.

She met his gaze then kissed him, murmuring, "Thank you, oh, thank you."

"She was really eager to meet you. Was a real nag about it."

Eden laughed and looked down as Hunter pushed his little finger into the baby's fist. The child latched on and Eden knew she'd trapped Hunter's heart. Over the tiny infant, their gazes locked, and Hunter leaned close, his lips brushing hers once, twice, then falling into a tender, loving kiss laced with new love and freshly found peace.

A swift, cool breeze stirred their hair, their clothes, the baby cooed. And Eden felt her sister's spirit touch them, warming them under the Indigo sun and showering them with a bright future.

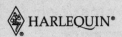
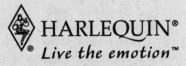

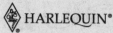